THE ANNALISE EXPERIMENT

By Willo Davis Roberts

THE ANNALISE EXPERIMENT
THE SNIPER
ACT OF FEAR
THE JAUBERT RING
EXPENDABLE
WHITE JADE

THE ANNALISE EXPERIMENT

WILLO DAVIS ROBERTS

PUBLISHED FOR THE CRIME CLUB
BY
DOUBLEDAY & COMPANY, INC.
GARDEN CITY, NEW YORK
1985

All of the characters in this book are fictitious, and any resemblance to actual persons, living or dead, is purely coincidental.

Library of Congress Cataloging in Publication Data

Roberts, Willo Davis.
The Annalise experiment.

I. Title.
PS3568.02478A75 1985   813'.54   84-21146
ISBN 0-385-19812-4
Copyright © 1985 by WILLO DAVIS ROBERTS
All Rights Reserved
Printed in the United States of America

First Edition

THE ANNALISE EXPERIMENT

1.

Silas Copetti slouched in the seat of the battered taxi, visored cap pulled down over his dark hair and shading gray eyes—steely gray eyes, Diana had laughingly called them, in the days when they could still laugh together—sucking the final infinitesimal drop of nicotine from the next-to-the-last cigarette of the day. Christ, he wished he could stop smoking the damned things. For a while, after each one, he'd think, hell, it ought to be easy to give them up. He was thirty-eight years old, in control of his own destiny, wasn't he?

Of course that was where the logic began to break down, almost before it had begun. Sure, he was in control. That's why he lived in a ratty three-room apartment while Diana had the house, and the T-bird, and Patty. Patty-cake, he'd always called her, and even though she now chided him for using a baby name, when she was seven years old, he knew she still liked it.

He was equally in control of his career life. Fourteen years on the San Cristobal P.D. down the drain, and now he played at being a private investigator while he really mostly paid his bills by driving a cab.

He sighed and ground out the butt in the ashtray. He felt conspicuous here on the street across from the gates to that exclusive convalescent hospital because it was on the edge of town and there wasn't much traffic on this street. What there was ran to Mercedes and Lincolns and Cadillacs; his beat-up old heap stood out like a thumb he'd just hit with a hammer.

There was a high wall around the place, brick, like the buildings inside which were scattered around on the manicured lawns. The gates stood open, wrought-iron, elaborately curlicued, with the name over them in the same ironwork: Forest Hills.

Sounded like a cemetery, he thought, not a hospital. Well, for some it was the last stop before the cemetery. Like Uncle Isadore.

He'd talked to Aunt Tillie night before last, when the entire clan had gathered to celebrate his mother's sixty-eighth birthday. The Copettis were great on birthdays. And any other holiday or excuse to get together. He'd enjoyed that, when he was head of his own family, though Diana had wearied of pasta dinners and screeching kids. He'd planned to take Patty with him on Sunday—after all, his mother was her grandmother—but Diana had forgotten the date.

"I'm sorry, Si. Honest to God, I just forgot, and bought tickets to the circus. I can't change them, they're sold out, and Sunday's the last day. I promised her, and she's been looking forward to it for weeks."

He gave her the benefit of the doubt, though Diana and his mother had never really enjoyed one another's company too much. If it had been anyone else's birthday, Silas wouldn't have gone himself, but it was more or less a command performance, under the circumstances. Lida Copetti would have been not only hurt but disgraced if her only son hadn't shown up for the occasion.

So he'd eaten spaghetti and four kinds of salad and hot buttery garlic bread, with cake and ice cream for dessert, and Aunt Tillie had cornered him while the younger women were doing the dishes.

"I wish you'd look into it, Si," the old lady said.

He stared down at her compassionately from his six-two superiority. He liked Aunt Tillie. She was a round, soft, gentle lady, and there'd never been any man in her life but Uncle Isadore.

"Honey," he said gently, "Uncle Izzy was seventy-six. He had a heart attack. It happens all the time."

"He never had anything wrong with his heart before. He just got out of the regular hospital, for heaven's sake. They did all kinds of tests on him, when he had his gallbladder out. They said he was fine, just needed a little bit more care than I could give him at home, because of that kidney infection he picked up." Her round chin firmed. "He might still be alive, if I'd insisted on bringing him home. Seventy-six isn't old, Si. Not these days. And he was in good health, until that gallbladder started acting up."

"Did they do an EKG?"

"I don't know, but the bills were tremendous. I'd think they'd have done everything, before they operated, just to be sure.

There's something . . . not right, Si. I just feel it in my bones. Something fishy about the way he died."

"Forest Hills is one of the best places in the county. Remember? You and Ma looked at a dozen places before you had him transferred there from San Cristobal General. You all agreed it was a classy place."

"Well, it did *look* nice. So clean, and none of that hospital smell, and the rooms didn't look that way, either. But he was so *thin*, he'd lost so much weight I would hardly have known him, and—" The old lady gazed at him tremulously, and he'd had to pat her on the shoulder.

"I'll see what I can do," he told her, and quelled the guilt that rose from the relief in her eyes.

So here he was, sitting watching for hell knew what, outside the fancy hospital where Uncle Isadore had died two and a half weeks ago. He didn't think there was anything peculiar about the old man's death. True, he'd been in excellent health for his age up to a month ago. But gallbladder surgery is tough on anybody, let alone old people, and then he'd picked up that damned kidney infection, so he ran a fever for a few days. All that took its toll. Naturally Izzy had lost weight when he was so sick and couldn't eat the way he usually did. It wasn't really a surprise that he'd had a fatal heart attack, no more of a surprise than the fact that Tillie couldn't let him go.

A figure emerged from the main building, directly ahead through the wrought-iron gates. It was a woman in a bright red skirt and jacket and carrying a matching purse that bumped against her thigh as she hurried toward him.

Just as she reached the gates, a city bus roared by without slowing. The girl's mouth opened in a distressed O as she stared after it.

She was pretty, Silas saw. Twenty-six or -seven, he estimated, with a slim figure. He guessed she'd had a recent weight loss, because the clothes were a little too loose on her. Her fair hair was caught back with some sort of barrette like Diana used.

His window was open, and he heard her swear. She looked across the street at the taxi, hesitated, then came briskly toward him, stooping to peer into the opposite window. "Excuse me, but is this cab taken?"

Silas straightened behind the wheel. "Well, yes, ma'am. My fare will probably be another twenty minutes or so."

"I just missed my bus. I have a dentist's appointment. It's only about three miles, but I can't walk it in time. Could you possibly drive me there? You could be back in less than twenty minutes."

"Sure. Jump in," Silas agreed, and reached back to open the rear door.

She wafted some nice fragrance toward him. "Thank you. Normally I have my car, but I'm having the brakes relined today, and I thought I could depend on the bus, only it was early. My dentist is just before you get to the Lakewood Mall, the west entrance."

Silas turned the key in the ignition. "You work in that place? Or just visiting?"

"Oh, I work there. I'm the receptionist," the girl said readily.

"Looks like a nice place, for a hospital."

"Oh, it is. I love working here. Except when somebody dies, of course. Though all the ones who have died have been old, and as Dr. Brogan says, everyone has to die sometime. It's up to our staff to see that they do it as comfortably as possible." She leaned back in the seat as Silas waited for a yellow Jaguar to go by.

It turned in between the hospital gates, however, driven by a man with a full head of silvery hair.

"Nice car," Silas observed, moving into traffic.

"Oh, yes, that's Dr. Brogan's," the girl said.

"Must be good business, running a hospital like this. I suppose it's an expensive place." He watched her in the rearview mirror, and saw her nod.

"Yes, but if you've ever seen other convalescent homes, you know it's worth it. I remember the one my grandfather was in— God, it was awful!"

Silas kept his tone noncommittal. "You work there long?"

"Eight months." The girl sighed, but she was smiling. "I'll only be working another two weeks. I'm getting married a week from Saturday."

"Congratulations." He slid the cab between a floral delivery van and a pickup loaded with trash, dodged an idiot in a blue Pinto who had suddenly decided to make a left turn from the wrong lane, and rechecked his passenger. "I'm sure he's a lucky guy."

"He thinks so," the girl said. "I've only known him for two

months, but that's long enough to know if you're in love or not, don't you think?"

He'd known Diana for more than a year before he'd married her, and they hadn't lasted to their tenth anniversary. "Sure," he told her. "It's nice he can support you. Lotta girls have to keep on working after they're married."

"I know. Zack doesn't want me to work, though. His hours are so irregular that if I was working too we'd hardly ever get to see each other, you know? There, that's Dr. Godey's office, in that building on the corner."

He brought the cab smoothly to the curb. "I suppose if you stayed on at a rest home for a long time, it would begin to get to you. People dying, I mean."

She was poised on the edge of the seat, handing over the fare. "Well, yes. Of course I don't work too much directly with the patients, so I don't get attached to them the way the nurses do, you know. Unless they get a lot of mail. I'm usually the one takes them their mail. Old people can be really interesting, you know? Dr. Brogan never minds if I visit with them for a few minutes. He says making them happy and comfortable is part of our job too."

He took the bill she offered and made change. She hesitated over it and handed back a quarter. "Nice fellow, this Dr. Brogan," he said. He wondered if this was the first time she'd ever taken a cab.

"Oh, my, yes. He's the nicest man I ever worked for. He really cares about people, even the ones who are old and dying. Thanks so much. I hope I didn't make you late for your other fare."

He watched her go up the walk to the dentist's office, then made a U-turn and headed back toward Forest Hills. He wasn't sure why. He certainly hadn't learned anything to make him think that there was anything peculiar about Uncle Isadore's death. Still, it was as good a place as any to sit until he got another fare, he supposed.

2.

Matthew Brogan slid the yellow Jaguar into the parking place reserved for him and turned off the ignition. He'd always had a passion for good cars; besides this one, which was admittedly an extravagance, he owned a pale blue Lincoln and a discreet dark gray BMW. The cars were part of his image, he rationalized; people expected an important man to play the part.

He didn't worry about locking the car when he got out. The security force—two men on duty per shift—could be trusted to see to its safety. Many of his patients were wealthy people; they had a right to know they were protected at all times, and besides, the uniformed officers impressed the relatives.

The whole place impressed the relatives. Hell, the place impressed *him,* and after nearly eight months you'd think he'd be used to it. There were thirty acres within the walls, mostly wooded except for the ten acres that housed the hospital itself, Aaron's laboratory, assorted outbuildings, and the condo where he and Aaron and the more important staff members had their living quarters. Eventually, Brogan intended to build himself a house apart from the condo; he'd picked out the spot, which needed only to be cleared of a few trees to be ideal. A big house, for entertaining and impressing people.

He had to laugh to himself, to think about Matthew Brogan impressing people. God forbid they should ever learn of his origins, although there was nothing wrong with overcoming adversity, after all. It was the American ethic, wasn't it? Rags to riches. Let them know he was a self-made man, but leave out the part about the alcoholic mother who brought home one man after another, and the father who had deserted wife and children before Matt was even old enough to remember him. Leave out the squalor in which he'd been reared, the cockroaches, the rats, the man coming to turn off the electricity because the bill hadn't been paid, the early brushes with the law when he ran with a gang, stealing hubcaps to peddle to that dirty old Sheffield for spending money.

Why was he thinking of that now? He paused on the ramp to look out over the grounds, noticing that Shelton was cutting the grass near the gates on the riding mower. Good investment, that. The old man could cover the grounds much more quickly, and the mower, too, was a prestigious symbol.

They were great on symbols, these rich people, he thought. He did not include himself in their number, though he was, by any standard, quite well-to-do. In his heart, though, he suspected that he would always be poor. He always remembered to squeeze the last of the toothpaste out of the tube, and to turn off the light when he left a room. Well, as the old saying went, take care of the pennies and the pounds would take care of themselves. At least early poverty hadn't made it impossible for him to enjoy the luxuries, now that they were within his grasp.

"Good morning, Doctor."

He turned to the bright, smiling young face. Janet Kowalski, one of the aides in a pastel pink uniform (he believed that the patients found it more cheerful), was coming down the ramp, pushing a wheelchair.

"Good morning, Janet. Good morning, Mrs. Hampton. Getting some of this lovely sunshine, I see. Very good for you."

The fat old woman in the wheelchair didn't return his smile. "They brought me prunes for breakfast again this morning. I've told them and told them, I *hate* prunes."

His blue eyes twinkled with amusement. "Well, I'll certainly speak to them about it. Apricots would probably do as well."

"I don't like apricots either. Why can't I just have my laxative, the way I always have?" the woman asked petulantly.

"Because natural laxatives, like fruit, are better for you. How about applesauce? Or a bowl of bran?"

Mrs. Hampton sighed heavily and changed the subject. "Nobody has been to see me for three days. When my daughter put me in here, she promised to visit regularly."

"Your daughter is a very busy lady," Brogan reminded her. "But perhaps Miss Miller can give her a call and let her know she's missed. In the meantime, why don't you join the others in the lounge? I believe there's a concert today, isn't there, Janet?"

"A group from the college," Janet confirmed. "At two o'clock."

"That modern music. Such a racket! And I never understand the words at all."

"Just as well, perhaps. Only it's chamber music today, if I remember correctly." He reached out to pat the puffy, liver-spotted hand. He believed very strongly in the power of touching, and, sure enough, the old woman's expression did soften. "Have a nice outing, Mrs. Hampton."

He went inside and, as he always did, took pleasure in this hospital that he had created. There was no institutional feeling, at least not in any of the places that the patients or their families could see. There were pastel-tinted walls, vast expanses of luxurious carpeting, paintings by well-known artists and talented young ones. The only concession to business, in the huge main lounge, was a small desk on the right as one entered through the front doors, with a white telephone on it.

Sylvia Miller was not seated there. It was too late for her to be delivering mail, Brogan thought, and then remembered that the receptionist had a dental appointment today.

"Good morning, Dr. Brogan."

"Good morning, Doctor."

Everyone spoke to him, respectfully, with affection, staff and patients alike. There were no patients in pajamas or dressing gowns; another of Brogan's firm beliefs was that a person was less likely to feel sick if he put on his clothes, even if he had to sit in a wheelchair.

Brogan himself always wore a suit. Today it was blue—he favored blue—which brought out the lighter shade of his eyes, and his silvery pompadour was, as usual, perfectly combed. The gold watch and heavy, square gold links in his cuffs were his only jewelry. He felt a doctor should have hands that looked clean, as well as being clean; it gave the patients confidence in him.

"Confidence is half the battle," he was wont to tell his staff. "If they don't trust us, they won't get better, or it will take longer. If they believe us when we say they're improving, chances are they will be."

There was never any doubt, with any of them, that they trusted

Matthew Brogan. He exuded self-confidence, and they absorbed it by osmosis.

Except for Aaron, of course.

Brogan lifted an affable hand to those across the room and turned to the left, toward his office. No, he'd never been able to pass any of his confidence on to his brother-in-law. He wondered, not for the first time, what Aaron Spaulding would have been like, had Lisa lived. He'd never known what his sister had seen in the skinny, unprepossessing fellow, although of course the man was brilliant. Still, it wasn't just brains that a woman usually took note of, and Aaron was nothing to look at.

Brogan's office was as attractive as the rest of the place. His own desk was massive—here the patients and relatives would expect some evidence that business was conducted—and there were yards of creamy-beige carpeting, walnut-paneled walls, and dark brown draperies across the windows that looked out over the grounds. On the surface of the gleaming desk stood only a small vase—a celadon porcelain from the Sung dynasty that was worth three times what he'd paid for the Jaguar—with a single yellow rosebud. Quiet, understated, elegant. Just what he'd dreamed of all those years when he'd tried to rouse his mother from a drunken stupor to remind her that she hadn't brought home any groceries and he and Lisa were hungry.

Vonda Busby was standing at the window, looking out to where the poplars were turning gold, leaves rippling and shifting in the breeze. She swiveled, smiling, and not for the first time he thought she was one of the handsomest nurses he'd ever seen in all his years in this business.

"Good morning," she said. "How did it go with the Lundstroms?"

"The old gentleman will be arriving tomorrow," Brogan said with satisfaction. "Kicking and screaming, probably, but I left a sedative to give him before they leave home. Room 204, do you think?"

"Very nice," Vonda agreed.

The phrase echoed in his mind. An apt description of the speaker, he thought. Her fair hair was cut short and waved gently around her face; her eyes were a deep and unusual shade of violet, and no infant ever had a softer, prettier skin. She wore her uniform with class, but the curves were there, all right, lush and remarkably firm, considering that she was thirty-four. Most women had lost their appeal for him by the time they were thirty.

"Sylvia's still at the dentist's, so I talked to Charlotte. She'd like you to call her," Vonda said.

Charlotte was his ex-wife. One of his ex-wives. He punched the proper button on the automatic dialing device. "Another crisis, I suppose?"

"The cost of Donald's orthodontic work, I think. The estimate was forty-two hundred dollars."

"Jesus Christ," Brogan muttered under his breath, and then, as the connection was made, "Char? I'm rather busy today, I'd appreciate it if you'd keep it short."

The nursing supervisor had not left the room. She stood watching him as he spoke with the mother of his son.

"I know that, Char. Well, I suppose we'll have to. Yes, of course, have him send the bills to me."

Brogan hung up with a grimace. "Wives, children," he said. "Sometimes I wish I'd had the sense to stop before I began."

Vonda Busby smiled slightly. "You know you don't mean that. You adore your children, all three of them."

"I adore them and deplore them, all at the same time," he told her. "And wives—well, I've stopped *that* nonsense, at least. It took me only fifty-two years to come to my senses, but there'll never be another wife to milk me dry. Dryer."

He made the statement deliberately. He knew Vonda had her eye on him; he'd seen that look on a woman's face too often not to recognize it. Not that he'd mind having an affair with her, should she prove amenable, but he meant it about not ever getting married again.

She was standing close enough to him so that he could reach out and run a finger up her bare arm. "How about having dinner with me tonight? My place?"

The smile perceptibly deepened. "I'd love to, Doctor." She lifted a finger of her own and brushed the cleft in his chin, the one each of his wives had once found irresistible. "In the meantime, would you like to see Mr. Crowley? He seems to require a regular dose of your bedside manner to keep him in line. He's causing trouble with the aides."

"Pinching bottoms again? Poor old fool."

"It's more than bottoms. He's taken to throwing things. Like his bedpan. After he's used it."

"Oh, lord. Well, I will have a talk with him. Oh, by the way, did you check the paper yet today? Did our ad come out without a misprint? It would be nice if they could get the goddamned telephone number right. Sylvia leaves in only two weeks, and I'd like her to have time to train a replacement."

Vonda's smile was serene. "I checked, and it's exactly as you dictated it."

"Good. I have to talk to Dr. Spaulding first, and then I'll descend upon Mr. Crowley. Seven o'clock, formal, all right?"

"Fine," Vonda agreed, and preceded him out of the office.

He cut across the grass, going to the laboratory. He didn't encourage shortcuts that would wear paths in the lawns, but once in a while he broke his own rules. The door stood open to the warm September day, and inside he heard Aaron's radio playing. Hard rock, of all things. The minute he stepped inside, Brogan reached over and switched it off.

His brother-in-law turned around after about thirty seconds. "Oh, Matt," he said vaguely.

Aaron Spaulding was forty-eight, but he looked older than Brogan's fifty-two. His dark hair was going thin on top, and he needed a haircut and a shampoo. He was six feet tall, and almost cadaverously thin; half the time he forgot to eat, as he forgot about getting a haircut. His deep-set dark eyes could be black with pain, as when Lisa had died, or lit by an inner fire when he talked about his work, but mostly they gave him the abstracted air of a man who doesn't realize where he is or what is happening. Though he had acknowledged Brogan's presence, Matt knew he was still engrossed in whatever he was doing with his test tubes.

"I've checked over Mrs. Hampton's records, and examined her as well. I think we might try her on the serum," Brogan suggested.

"Oh? Hampton, is it?"

"Amelia Hampton. Room 230." He didn't know why he always gave the full name and the room number. Aaron never remembered. He'd always have to check with the nurse on duty. But he would remember to bring the serum. "Make it tomorrow, all right?"

"Fine," Aaron Spaulding said. After a three-minute silence during which Dr. Spaulding busied himself with several beakers, Brogan turned and walked quietly away.

3.

"Sammie, hurry up," Erin Randall told her eight-year-old daughter, "or you'll be late. I told you, I can't drive you to school anymore, not until I get another job. I can't afford the gas."

The little girl sat in the middle of the living-room rug, tying her shoes. Her pleated plaid skirt was slid up so that she unself-consciously displayed her Wonder Woman Underoos. "Mom, am I going to go and stay with Grandma Randall?"

Erin swallowed and kept her voice level. "I don't think so, honey. I think it's best if we stay together, don't you? Now that Daddy's gone . . ." She had to swallow again, and she wondered how long it would take—forever?—before she could talk about Ted without this excruciating rush of emotion. But already it was fading, she decided. "Come on, here's your sweater."

Samantha stood up and shrugged into the sweater. "Grandma says you can't afford to feed me."

"You haven't gone hungry yet, have you? Here's your lunch." Ruth meant well, Erin thought, but she wished her mother-in-law would be more careful about what she said in front of Sammie. Even if what she said was true.

She stared down at the child, caught, as she often was, in a sense of wonder that she could have produced such exquisite beauty. Erin's own coppery waves had combined with Ted's straight fair hair to produce in Sammie pale red-gold curls around a deceptively cherubic face, and a complexion unblemished except by a sprinkling of freckles across the short nose. No, even the freckles weren't a blemish, for they added to Sammie's charm.

"Okay, I'm ready. Listen, Mom"—the little upturned countenance grew serious—"if you need me to go to Grandma's, I'll go. I don't mind changing schools, really."

Erin hugged her daughter and shooed her out the door. "Thank you, honey, but we'll manage. See you this afternoon, okay?"

The apartment was quiet after Sammie had gone. Erin stood for a moment leaning against the door, wondering if she'd spoken the truth. Could she keep things together if something didn't turn up soon? She loved Ruth Randall, as much as she'd loved her own mother, but Ruth was too old to take on a young child, and besides, then Sammie would be deprived not only of her father but her mother as well.

Ruth's words hung in her memory. "You could both move in with me, Erin. I've plenty of room, and it would be so much cheaper for you."

Cheaper, yes. But it would mean relinquishing her freedom, and she couldn't bring herself to do that. Not unless there was absolutely no other choice.

She looked around the apartment, the one they'd moved to when the bank foreclosed on the house—the house that would have been paid for when Ted died if he hadn't forgotten to make the payment on the insurance. The same way he'd forgotten to make the payment on his life insurance.

The little wave of bitterness swept over her, and with it, guilt. Ted was gone, crushed under a truck when its brakes gave way on a hill, and she tried not to resent the things he had done—or failed to do—when he was alive.

Handsome, charming, and totally undependable. Well, she'd known that for years, hadn't she? How many times had she discovered letters still in his coat pocket, unmailed, days after payments were due? She'd known better, yet she'd entrusted the checks for the insurance to him. They were still in his pocket when his belongings were returned to her from the hospital. They had been there for three weeks, and the grace periods had expired. Ted had left her with nothing but the $312 dollars they'd had in the bank, and more than that owing on current debts.

There wasn't even room in this place to pace the floor satisfactorily, she thought, frustrated. She'd put most of their things in storage in Ruth Randall's garage, grateful that she didn't have to pay for it, and brought these few things here: the twin beds from Sammie's room, for they now shared the single bedroom, which wasn't large enough for a king-size bed, anyway; the smallest of the dressers, the couch and matching platform rocker and Ted's recliner, which were all that would fit into the living room, the dinette set they'd had in the kitchen, because the dining-room suite was much too large for this place.

She'd thought maybe having familiar furniture around would make the apartment seem more like home. Instead, the impression was one of discord, disorientation. Nothing belonged here, and there was no harmony.

Erin picked up the breakfast dishes and put them in the sink to soak in sudsy water while she looked at the morning paper. The headlines were the usual horror stories of domestic and international crises and catastrophes. She skimmed the headlines, skipped the comics, and went directly to the classified ads.

God, if only she were qualified for something, she thought. If only Ted hadn't been adamant about her not working. She was taking a computer class at the junior college, but it would be months before she was proficient enough to think about work in that line. Right now she had two part-time jobs, both of them paying minimum wage and just barely enabling her to keep up the rent and buy bread and peanut butter. She knew she ought to be glad the car was paid for, so she wasn't limited to looking for jobs on the city bus lines, but . . . there was that ad again, the one she'd tried to answer last week, only to be told by an irate householder that she had the wrong number.

Receptionist. Must have pleasant, friendly personality, and good appearance. Prefer woman between twenty and thirty. Excellent working conditions and salary to right party. Call 847-7310.

Was that the same phone number? Or had they corrected it? Erin rose and went to the stack of newspapers she hadn't yet carried over to her mother-in-law's to be burned in the fireplace. She pawed through them until she found the one she wanted, folded open at the correct page and with the ad circled. Yes, the numbers were now transposed from the ones that had been there earlier.

Between twenty and thirty. Were they allowed to stipulate age these days? Wasn't it discriminatory? Still, unless someone complained to the proper government agency, who would interfere? Could she pass for thirty? She stared into the tiny mirror that had been placed over the sink in lieu of a window. Well, she was only two years older, and she still looked pretty good except for the dark smudges under her eyes. Smudges that came from lying awake worrying about what she was going to do, how she was going to manage.

Impulsively Erin picked up the phone and dialed the number.

"Good morning. Forest Hills."

What was that? A mortuary? It didn't matter, Erin decided. The important thing was a full-time job, an adequate paycheck. "Good morning, I'm calling about your ad for a receptionist," she said.

"I'm sorry, Dr. Brogan wants to do all the interviewing himself, and he hasn't come in yet. Would you mind calling back around eleven?" The voice was crisply professional.

"Not at all," Erin said, though disappointment was crushing. How many other people would also be calling back then? She hung up, then evaluated the little she'd learned. A doctor? Doctors usually made enough to pay decent salaries, didn't they?

The telephone directory was in the drawer in the telephone table, and she spread it out and flipped through the pages. There it was: Forest Hills Convalescent Hospital, 1400 Beverly Boulevard.

A convalescent hospital. Her expectations diminished somewhat. What little she knew of such institutions wasn't promising. Still, wasn't Beverly Boulevard out where the golf course was, the San Cristobal County Club? She'd driven past that, and she remembered it as being rather an elegant neighborhood.

Well, there was nothing else that sounded promising. At least two of the jobs still listed in the paper had already been taken; she'd called them before. The agencies had three that might be possibilities, but she couldn't afford the fee of one month's salary, so that didn't do her any good.

Beverly Boulevard. What would this Dr.—Brogan, was it?—think if she turned up in person, rather than setting up an appointment?

The more she thought about it, the more urgent it seemed. There were no specific duties listed, but being a receptionist usually entailed answering the phone and greeting visitors, didn't it? Maybe a little light typing. She couldn't compete with those who did ninety words a minute, but she was accurate at about fifty-five, and she was picking up speed working on the computers in night school. Maybe, for a receptionist, that would be enough.

Without even having consciously made the decision, Erin moved toward the bathroom and turned on the shower.

It *was* an elegant neighborhood. Big houses, set well back from the street, separated by woods or fences. And there was Forest Hills, the name spelled out over the gates so that she didn't even need the number to confirm it. She was surprised they'd let anybody operate a convalescent hospital here, because of the proximity of those quarter- to half-million-dollar houses. Forest Hills sat on an extensive piece of ground, though, and if it didn't create a traffic problem perhaps surrounding property owners wouldn't find much to object to.

She eased the six-year-old Camaro between the fancy gates and found a parking space that was marked VISITOR. Off to one side, on a black-topped path, an attendant in a pale green uniform pushed a wheelchair with an old man in it. Ahead of them, near the edge of the woods, a young woman and an older one strolled, each with another attendant, one in pale blue, the other in yellow.

Not, Erin thought, getting out of the car, quite what she'd thought of in terms of convalescent hospitals.

When she entered the door, her expectations were upgraded once more. Sculptured carpeting in two tones of green, couches and comfortable chairs, bookcases flanking a massive brick fireplace, soft music from some unseen source. Erin turned toward the desk, where a neat sign said SYLVIA MILLER, RECEPTIONIST.

The blond girl in the red suit smiled brightly at her. "Good morning. May I help you?"

"Yes." Was it a mistake to have come in person? Erin hoped desperately that she hadn't blown it. "I've come about the job that was advertised in the paper this morning."

There was no discernible disapproval in Sylvia Miller's face. "Of course. One moment, please, and I'll see if Dr. Brogan can see you now. Otherwise, we'll make an appointment for you to come back." The smile seemed genuinely welcoming, and Erin took heart.

Two minutes later, Sylvia ushered her into an office down the hall, and the man behind the massive desk stood up, smiling.

His handshake was warm and firm. "I'm Matt Brogan," he said.

He was magnificent, Erin thought, even if he must be past fifty.

That silvery hair with every wave in place, the height, the trim figure in an expensive blue suit exuded authority and personality.

"I'm Erin Randall." She gave up the idea of lying about her age; those blue eyes were too observant, too sharp. "I'm afraid I'm past the age you specified, by about two years, but I think I'd make a good receptionist, and I need the job."

He'd noted the rings on her left hand. "Sit down, Mrs. Randall. We won't quibble about two years. Let's talk about you, what you like to do, why you need a job."

She heard herself telling him things she hadn't told any of the other prospective employers. Like having lost her husband nine months ago, and after Ted the house and all security—though she didn't mention that the security had not been all that great even when her husband was alive—and about Samantha, and that she liked to read thrillers and historical novels, and jogged a little for exercise, and so far hadn't had to diet to keep her figure. She wasn't certain how that last had come out, except that he'd asked about her general health and her eating habits.

"We believe that what we eat has a good deal to do with our health, and it's important that we don't have staff members who eat candy bars, for instance, in front of the patients. We like our staff to set a good example for our patients and their relatives."

"This is a beautiful place," Erin told him sincerely. "Not at all what I'd expected of a rest home. Or must I say convalescent hospital?"

He shrugged. "It serves both functions. Many of our patients are here because they are elderly, perhaps sick, and cannot be properly managed at home. A few of them are young and come for true convalescence, during which they will be restored to good health and full activity. One of our primary requirements in an employee, Mrs. Randall, is a genuine caring attitude toward our patients, including the occasionally irascible one. Have you ever worked with sick or elderly people?"

"No," Erin admitted. "But I've always gotten along well with elderly relatives. And I took care of my own mother for several months when she was in the terminal stages of cancer."

He nodded that silvery head. "Very sad. We have some cancer patients, of course. Our hope is to keep them as comfortable as possible, and as happy. We do this at least partly by maintaining a cheerful staff. You may have noticed the lack of sterile white uniforms, except for our nursing supervisor, Miss Busby. Do you think it would bother you to deal with these patients?"

"I don't think so," Erin said truthfully.

Dr. Brogan leaned back in his chair and regarded her with a smile. "All right. Why don't you fill out this form—" He produced it from a drawer and slid it across his desk. "You may sit out in the main lounge to do it, and give the papers to Miss Miller when they're completed. I'll want to do a background check on you before I make my decision. Are you bondable?"

"As far as I know, I am." Her pulses had increased; she was sure, from the way he was looking at her, that he would hire her.

"Very well." He stood up, and she rose too, holding the forms. "I like a woman with initiative, and you have that, or you wouldn't have come here instead of settling for a telephone call. We'll let you know, one way or the other, by Friday. How will that be?"

"Fine," Erin said. "And I thank you for seeing me."

And then, as she turned to go, her elbow caught the vase on the edge of the desk. She grabbed for it, catching the vase before it went over the edge, but the water spilled onto desk and carpet, and the yellow rosebud landed across one of her black pumps. She stared at the mess in dismay.

"Don't worry about it," Dr. Brogan said, moving around the desk. He righted the vase, stooped to retrieve the rose and stuck it back where it belonged, then took a box of tissues from the desk and mopped at the water. He even smiled. "That will be one of your jobs," he told her, "putting a fresh flower in that vase every morning."

He walked to the door and held it open for her, with no further word of farewell. How could she convince him that she was not ordinarily clumsy? Better to say nothing, she thought, than botch things any more by saying the wrong thing. Yet he'd said, *that will be one of your jobs.* He meant to hire her, didn't he? She thought he did.

She spoke briefly to Sylvia Miller, at the desk, then sat in one of the chairs near the receptionist's to fill out the forms. They were standard: name, address, dependents, spouse, social security number, job history, the health history perhaps a bit more complete than most. That was only to be expected, working in a hospital, she supposed. They even wanted height and weight, and to know if she'd gained or lost weight during the past year.

A ten-pound loss, she thought, during those weeks after Ted's death when she hadn't felt like eating. She put them back on, though, after a few months, and they were about right now for her five feet, seven inches. She wrote *no* after the question and finished up quickly, handing the papers over to Sylvia.

"Dr. Brogan said someone would call me on Friday, one way or the other," she said.

The other girl nodded, smiling. "They will. Dr. Brogan always keeps his promises. Good luck; I hope you get the job."

"Thank you," Erin said. She walked out the front door, which was held open for her by a man in uniform. She felt more optimistic than she had in some time.

4.

He had a legitimate fare in the neighborhood this time, a stout matron who lived in one of the fancy houses half a block from Forest Hills. Silas dropped her off and cruised back along Beverly Boulevard; he decided that directly opposite those gates was as good a place as any to eat his lunch.

He had finished his sandwich and was starting on the apple when the girl came out of the hospital door and cut across the lawn toward the parking area. A swirl of yellow and brown leaves lifted around her feet, and Silas watched her appreciatively.

Great legs, he thought. The wind caught her skirt, and she made a halfhearted effort to hold it down. Yes, definitely a ten on legs.

She unlocked an old green Camaro, turning so that he got a fairly good look at the rest of her. Pretty, he thought. No, stunning was more accurate. Coppery red hair in a waving cap, and an exceptional face.

She backed out of the parking slot and headed toward him, paying no attention to the old taxi across the street. A closer look at her face confirmed his initial impression, and he memorized her license number automatically, without conscious thought. Old habits die hard.

He finished the apple, started to throw the core out the window, then sighed and dropped it into the paper bag that still held one limp sandwich.

It was pointless, sitting around here. Even if there was anything to find out about what went on at Forest Hills, his chances of learning any of it by watching the front of the main building were remote. He put the cab in gear and headed back downtown.

How long had it been since he'd pushed through the double doors at Smitty's? Only a couple of times, Silas thought, since he'd left the force. It was a cop's bar, at least this time of night, and when he was no longer a cop, he no longer felt at home there.

He didn't feel at home now, though it was all familiar enough. The air was heavy with smoke and buzzed with low conversation and an occasional raucous burst of laughter. Smitty, squat and bald, was behind the bar; he saw Silas and lifted a hand in greeting.

"Long time no see, fella. What'll you have?"

Had Smitty forgotten his name already? Silas slid a bill across the bar. "Gimme an Oly, I guess."

"Your buddy's in the back booth," Smitty said. "Grady. Waiting for somebody. How you been, Si?"

"Tolerable," Silas conceded, feeling better. "Give me another one for Grady."

He carried the two glasses toward the rear of the dimly lighted room. He saw Rogers and Katolik at a table, deep in conversation. Rogers looked up and saw him, and waved, and then Katolik waved too. Silas nodded but didn't slow down.

Frank Grady's wide mouth spread in a grin when the beer was put down before him. "Son of a bitch. Where'd you come from?"

He didn't bother to answer. "How's it going, Frank? You making any progress with Littleton?"

"Nah. She got transferred over to the Sheriff's Department three months ago. We got a new dispatcher, Cheryl Williams. Five two, a hundred and five, blond, and blue-eyed." He took a long swig of the beer and grinned. "I think I'm making progress there, but the competition is keen."

"It always is," Si said, sliding into the booth opposite his old partner. "How are the kids?"

Grady shrugged. "Okay. Pat's taken on a live-in boyfriend, though. I don't think that's such a good example for kids, but what the hell? I don't have any say about what she does anymore."

About a third of the San Cristobal force consisted of divorced men, and half the rest of them were divorced and remarried. Marriage fatalities were a bigger risk than getting shot, among cops.

"I heard you worked for Henry Lewis, finding that kid of his."

Silas drank deeply before he replied. "Yeah. I think he'd have been happier if I hadn't found her. Now he knows what she is. Before, he could pretend he didn't."

They made small talk for a few minutes, before Silas introduced the subject that was on his mind. He didn't expect anything to come of it, but he wanted to put it to rest, to be able to assure Tillie that there had been nothing suspicious about old Isadore's death.

"You know anything about a Dr. Brogan, runs a rest home or something out on Beverly Boulevard? Forest Hills?"

Grady responded readily. "I know where it is. Classy joint, expensive as hell, I understand. The mayor put his mother there."

"What about this Brogan?"

Grady shrugged and drank again. "Well thought of, as far as I know."

"Could you poke around and see if there's anything, any hint of scandal? About the hospital, I mean, not just the doctor. Uncle Isadore died there a couple of weeks ago. My aunt thinks maybe there was something fishy about it."

"Yeah? Like what? He was an old guy, wasn't he?"

"Seventy-six. They said it was a heart attack, and it probably was, but I want to tell her I looked into it. No suspicious deaths out there that you know of?"

Grady shook his head. He was two years younger than Silas, lean and good-looking, with sandy hair and a small mustache. "Not a whisper of anything about the place, but I'll take a look for you."

"Thanks. I'd appreciate it. And oh, by the way, run down a license number for me, will you? MBS 734."

They chewed the fat for another five minutes, and then Grady stood up. "Hi, Cheryl. This is my old partner, Si Copetti."

Silas stood up too, making room for the girl. She was very attractive, just as Grady had described her. "Hi, Cheryl. I'm just leaving," Silas told her, and didn't stick around any longer. It only reminded him that when he went home it was to an unmade bed and breakfast dishes in the sink, in an apartment where no one cared, one way or the other.

Smitty waved as he headed for the door. "So long, Copetti."

At least the goddamned bartender hadn't forgotten him, for what that was worth.

He didn't see Grady for three days. Two of them he spent following the wife of a guy who hoped to catch her in bed with another man, and got his money's worth, complete with a Polaroid shot of the two of them coming out of a motel. The third day Silas drove cab, stayed busy, and dropped in again at Smitty's around nine, after a twelve-hour day.

Grady wasn't there, but he arrived ten minutes later, and they carried a pair of beers to a rear booth. Willie Nelson was singing the blues on the jukebox, and the noise level was high enough to indicate that most of the patrons had been drinking for a while.

"I didn't get you a hell of a lot," Grady said, going straight to the point. "Matthew Brogan, M.D., is a local boy made good. Has two ex-wives, both living in two-hundred-thousand-dollar homes; one of them has one kid, a boy of seventeen, and the other has twelve- and fourteen-year-old daughters. Private schools, music lessons, Country Club memberships all around."

He paused to light a cigarette, offering the pack across the table, and after an imperceptible hesitation, Silas accepted one.

"He was on the staff at County General for two years, excellent record, went into private practice with the Gould Group. He's said to be competent, and the ladies like his bedside manner." Grady held up a hand. "Not to be construed as *in* bed manner, though now that he's divorced he seems to see a variety of young females. If he's having an affair—or affairs—he's discreet about them."

"That's an expensive-looking setup he has. He earn the money to pay for that, looking down sore throats and palpating bellies?"

"No, Dr. Brogan had a little luck. Maybe he made his own luck. Anyway, Forest Hills was an estate, belonged to Charles and Myra Conrad, the ones who owned Conrad Lumber. Charles died of complications of diabetes, about six years ago. His widow enjoyed poor health, as they say, and came to depend heavily on Dr. Brogan. When she died, her will left the entire estate to her doctor."

"No kidding. Any hint of undue influence there?"

"Nope." Grady blew a haze of smoke between them. "Of course you never know for sure, but the old lady *was* sick, and Dr. Brogan attended her faithfully and eased her last days. The Conrads had no children surviving them, only a couple of cousins they detested. Before she changed her will to make Brogan the beneficiary, she was leaving it all to a home for stray cats or something. This way, he was able to turn the estate into a rest home, give up his general practice to run the hospital, and set his brother-in-law up with a laboratory where he's doing research of some kind. Cancer, maybe. His wife—Brogan's sister—died of cancer."

Silas made a snorting sound. "The way everybody thinks this Brogan is a saint, there's *got* to be something fishy about him."

Grady laughed. "Well, he may be a saint, but he charges earthly prices. I couldn't turn up any dirt on him at all, other than that he likes to be surrounded by pretty ladies, and it's a good thing *that* ain't a crime."

Silas scowled and finished off his beer. "Yeah. Oh, what about that license? Get me a make on that?"

"Sure. The car's registered to Theodore and Erin Randall, 1120 Fir Street, Apartment Four. That do anything for you?"

"Yeah. I might have known a woman who looked that good would be married," Silas said, and listened again to Grady's laughter.

He went out into the night, feeling a bit of a nip to the air, suggesting that summer was coming to an end. And what difference did it make to him?

He remembered what it had been like, once, coming home from a job he loved, even when he hated it, to a pretty wife, a delightful daughter who ran to leap into his arms, a dog that wagged a stubby tail when he heard the car, a house that smelled of roasting meat or chocolate chip cookies.

Shit, Silas thought, and kicked a beer can off the sidewalk into the gutter.

5.

From his bedroom the old man could hear them talking, although they pretended to lower their voices so that he would not. Ernie Denton was eighty-two, and without his glasses on couldn't have recognized his own hand, but his hearing wasn't gone yet. Sometimes he thought they pretended that it was, just so they could say those things they didn't want to say to his face, yet wanted him to know.

"How's he taking it?" his son-in-law had asked, and Paula, his own daughter, had spoken as if he were nothing.

"He's furious, just as I expected, but I've told him it's what we have to do. God, Neal, I can't take any more. We have to put him in that place. I wish I could make him understand!"

He understood, all right. They were tired of him. They were ashamed of him. He'd heard her say it, right out.

"I'm so embarrassed when anyone comes," Paula had told her husband. "Daddy looks so . . . so *gross*. He's so fat, and he eats like an animal, and just the way he breathes is enough to kill any conversation. You can't hear yourself over it."

"Yes, well, we're doing the right thing," Neal said self-righteously on the other side of the wall. "You want me to stay here in the morning until you get him in the car? Maybe it would be best to get an ambulance, after all."

"Oh, honey, I wish you would stay, just until we leave. But I don't know about the ambulance. It's one more thing to upset him. It'll seem more like he's going to a hospital instead of a rest home, won't it?"

"Maybe you're right. Did you get all the arrangements made?"

"Yes. Dr. Brogan came here and talked to me. I know it's terribly expensive, but I couldn't bear to put Daddy in any of those other places we looked at. They were so depressing. I wish I could make him see that it's because we care about him, not that we're trying to get rid of him, but he yelled at me, swore at me . . ."

The voices diminished, as if they were going away from him. Damn them both, the old man thought, heaving his bulk about on the bed. Expensive, hell, yes, that was nice of them, sending him to an expensive place. As if it wasn't his own money was going to pay for it. They'd already gone to court and Paula had had him declared incompetent, just because of those goddamned trains. As if a man didn't have a right to spend his own money for trains if he wanted to.

Come right down to it, his money had paid for this goddamned house. He'd started the business that his son-in-law now ran, and what had Neal paid him for it? Nothing! They'd just eased him out, slick as a whistle, and now they let him have an "allowance" that he wasn't even permitted to spend the way he wanted to.

His anger made him cough, and he struggled for breath and flailed around until his hand made contact with the bell on the bedside table. He hit it several times before anybody came.

Paula's pale blue eyes were wide and apprehensive as she held the glass for him to drink, poking the pill into his mouth before he'd even stopped coughing, so it was a wonder he didn't choke to death on it. Maybe that was what she wanted, just to get rid of him, once and for all.

"Daddy, try to calm down. Don't get so upset. You know it isn't good for you."

She was an old woman, he thought. All that gray in her hair, and going soft and plump. Her hands had blue veins in the backs of them, the hands she'd always taken such pride in; he'd told her, once, how foolish it looked to wear all those rings when her hands were so ugly now, and all she'd done was cry. Big, messy tears that plowed furrows down her cheeks and washed away her makeup.

"I'll bring you a sleeping pill," she told him now, "so you can get a good night's rest."

"I don't want any goddamned sleeping pill," he said hoarsely. Yet when she brought it, he swallowed it obediently, because he didn't want to lie here awake in the darkness all night, thinking about that place they were sending him to. He knew about rest homes. What did they think he was, an idiot?

Rest homes. They were where they sent people to die, when

they were of no use anymore. Goddamn them, he thought in impotent fury, and lashed out with a hand, before the drug could take effect, to send the lamp crashing against the wall.

He watched with a reasonable amount of satisfaction as Paula picked up the pieces and dumped them in the wastebasket, and wondered how she could cry those crocodile tears when he knew she didn't really care at all.

Erin recognized the voice at once.
"Mrs. Randall? This is Sylvia Miller at Forest Hills."
"Yes, hello." Hope made her catch her breath.
"Dr. Brogan asked me to call you and see if you could come to work on Monday. At nine?"
Relief and joy flooded through her. "Yes, I can." She wouldn't be able to give much notice at either the bowling alley or the restaurant, but they always had girls applying for jobs in both places. She couldn't pass this up in order to give them two weeks notice.
"Good. I'm sure you'll have time to learn everything before I leave." The tone grew warmer. "Dr. Brogan is marvelous to work for. I think you'll like working here as much as I have."
"I know I will," Erin said, and hung up in a sort of daze. It occurred to her that she hadn't even asked what the salary was, but what did it matter? It had to be more than what she was earning now, and it would be daytime work, mostly while Sammie was in school. She wouldn't have to leave her with Ruth on the nights she was on duty at the alleys, and she wondered if she should drop out of her computer classes on Tuesday nights, so she could be home with Sammie more.
"No," she said aloud, "maybe I better keep on with the classes. Being trained on computers ought to qualify me for a better job than receptionist eventually. I *knew* he liked me, though."
For a few seconds she considered the possibility that Dr. Brogan was a womanizer who picked his employees for, first, their looks, and, second, their receptivity to his advances. Almost at once, she dismissed the idea. Sylvia Miller certainly hadn't sounded like a girl who'd been coerced into an unwelcome affair with her boss; she was planning to be married. And Dr. Brogan, with his looks and his money, wouldn't have to hire female employees for his personal gratification.

The significance of that phone call swept over her, and Erin twirled around the kitchen. She had a job. With any luck, she'd be able to take care of herself and Sammie just fine now.

Maybe, she thought, checking the cash in her purse, they could afford to eat out tonight, at Sammie's favorite place: the McDonald's a block down the street.

She grinned, anticipating her daughter's delight.

"I checked it all out, Aunt Tillie," Silas told her. "Everybody says this Dr. Brogan is a great guy, a good doctor. He signed the death certificate, says it was a heart attack, and I couldn't find anything to suggest it wasn't. It's true the EKG at San Cristobal General didn't show any problem, but that doesn't mean he couldn't have had a coronary a few weeks later. He'd been subjected to a lot of additional stress by then. Forest Hills has the best reputation of any place in the area. The only thing I'm curious about is how you paid for it; it sounds like it doesn't take Medicare patients."

"Oh, they'll take Medicare, if you're there for something that Medicare covers," Tillie said. "Only they don't cover custodial care, you know. The patient has to need professional nursing care, not just aides looking after them. But of course you have to pay the difference between Medicare and the actual cost."

"So how did you pay for it?"

The old lady lifted her chin defiantly. "I borrowed on the house. It seemed like the best place to put him, and I wanted him to have the best."

Silas was silent, appalled. Tillie licked her lips.

"It's all right, Si. It was a small loan, and the boys have said they'll buy the house from me, and I'll take turns living with each of them, so it will come out all right. I don't think I'll mind staying a couple of months a year with each of them. After all, when you have six sons, you don't need to make any of them tired of you."

He patted her shoulder. "I don't guess they'd get tired of you anyway, honey. All you have to do is whip up a batch of your lasagna once in a while to keep everybody happy."

He was relieved that she'd accepted it, that she didn't continue to insist that there was something odd about how Uncle Isadore had died. He had a new case, another job of tracing down a runaway, and it would probably be just as dirty as the last one; after all, there wasn't much in the way of choices for a sixteen-year-old girl out on the streets, but it was a job, he'd handle it as impersonally as he could (sometimes he had to work to keep from imagining his own Patty in such a situation), and he'd get paid for it. He wasn't sure he'd ever make enough as a P.I. to fully support himself *and* pay child support—thank God they hadn't made him come up with alimony too—so he could quit driving the cab, but maybe it didn't matter.

He didn't have anybody to consider but himself, and his own needs were few. He went home from Aunt Tillie's and stuck a TV dinner in the microwave, eating it while watching a rerun of "Hill Street Blues."

The San Cristobal *Record* carried an obituary that evening.

Died, James Gregor, age 82, of natural causes. Survived by a cousin, Elsie Packard, and two nephews of this city. No services will be held.

Silas Copetti skimmed the statistics before he went to bed, but the name meant nothing to him. There was no mention of the fact that James Gregor had recently been a patient at Forest Hills.

Matt Brogan was entertaining Vonda Busby that evening, and did not read the *Record* at all. The maid disposed of the paper in the morning, and the doctor never saw it. He would have recognized the name.

Aaron Spaulding never read newspapers. The headlines did not interest him, nor did sports scores or comics. The last obituary that had held any significance for him was that of his beloved wife, two years previously. It is doubtful that he would have recognized the name of the deceased, for he seldom remembered names. But in this case, he should have remembered it.

6.

Erin loved the job at Forest Hills.

She'd been uncertain what to wear that first day. Finally she chose a tan skirted suit and an orange and brown figured blouse with a bow at the neck, and the boots Ted had given her for her last birthday, soft brown ones with enough heel to flatter her legs yet comfortable to walk in.

"Very nice," Dr. Brogan said, appraising her. "Sylvia will take you around, introduce you to everyone, see that you know where supplies are, meet the patients when she delivers the mail. Oh, and we didn't talk salary, did we?"

She left his office in a state of euphoria. She'd better wait a few weeks, anyway, to make sure the job and the salary was stable, and then she'd look for a nicer apartment. She supposed she'd better stay in the same school district so as not to disrupt Sammie's life again.

"I'm surprised you're leaving," she told Sylvia, accepting the cup of coffee the other girl had brought to the reception desk. "It's a remarkable salary for a receptionist. Or is there something more difficult than is usual?"

"Oh, no." Sylvia sipped at her own beverage. "It's only that Doctor pays well because he wants everyone to be happy here, to *stay*. Of course I *thought* I'd stay forever, when I came here, you know. It's the best job I ever had. I felt so *guilty*, telling him I was leaving to get married. It took me a whole week to get up enough nerve to do it, and then he was so sweet about it. He said, 'Why, of course I understand,' and I nearly cried."

"And you've been here how long? Eight months?"

"Yes. Ever since the place opened. Virtually everybody's been here that long. The only one, besides me, to leave was Mrs. Masterson, the head bookkeeper. She had a stroke, so they had to replace her." Sylvia put down her cup and fiddled with a pencil. "I never dreamed I'd be leaving to get married. Zack is the only boyfriend I ever had, and I'm twenty-eight years old." She smiled, twisting the diamond ring on her engagement finger. "I suppose you had plenty of boyfriends all your life. I knew Doctor would hire you unless you turned out to be a drug addict or something, you're so gorgeous. I've always been so ugly."

"Ugly?" Erin echoed, astonished. "But you're very pretty, Sylvia! Surely people must have told you that!"

"I wasn't pretty, before. Not when I came here. I'm surprised Dr. Brogan hired me, actually, because he likes people around him who are attractive. He always acts as if everyone's beautiful, but he *did* counsel me about my diet. He's not in private practice anymore, but if any of the staff need medical advice, he'll give it to you. At no charge. And there's hospitalization, that's part of the fringe benefits. I'll have to have you fill out these forms, for the insurance." She groped in the filing drawer in her desk and brought them out. "You can do that anytime. It won't take effect for thirty days."

She closed the drawer and yelped in pain, then sucked at a reddened finger. "I don't know what's the matter with me. I'm so awkward these days, so clumsy. I didn't use to be. I guess I'm nervous. There's so much to do, even though we're having a small home wedding. Premarital jitters, or something."

Erin nodded in understanding. "I think a lot of women feel that way."

"Did you?"

Erin wondered if they shouldn't be getting on with learning the job, but if Sylvia wanted to just talk, it was up to her. And maybe the doctor had asked to do that, to put Erin at ease, or to find out more about her.

"Ted and I eloped, so I didn't have time to get very nervous," Erin admitted. "I didn't know it was the night before the wedding until after it was over."

Sylvia sighed. "Sometimes I think we'd have been smarter to elope. Save a lot of trouble. But I know it's going to be a nice wedding. Come on, here's the mail. We'll sort it out, and I'll show you around while we deliver it, okay?"

The main building had four stories. "It was a private house once," Sylvia said, explaining the generous size of the rooms. "Can you imagine, having a sixty-foot living room? And wait'll you see the bathrooms. It's really like living in a good hotel, more than a hospital. Dr. Brogan encourages the patients to come down and eat in the dining room—we'll go back there later, meals are included in your benefits, did I tell you that?—although of course some of them aren't well enough for that. We'll use the elevator. That had to be put in before the place opened, a big one so we can move beds if necessary. There's another one at the back of the building."

The elevator rose silently, smoothly. Sylvia seemed almost a compulsive talker. When there wasn't anything to explain, she talked about herself. In the elevator she said her Zack was so good-looking, and he had a good job. He didn't want her to work, he said, because he hoped she'd have babies right away.

"Well, when you're twenty-eight, you don't want to waste too much time, do you?"

Erin said she supposed not.

"I saw on your application form that you have one little girl."

"Yes. Sammie, for Samantha. She's eight."

"And she's all you have?"

"Yes. Just one. She's plenty for me to handle," Erin said, smiling a little. She wasn't going to go into any explanations of her own, of how she'd wanted several children but had come to the reluctant conclusion that it would be better not to have any more because of the way Ted was, always changing jobs, always keeping her frantic about money. She'd loved him, she really had, but there was no denying he was not the best provider in the world.

"I'd like a girl, first. And then maybe two boys," Sylvia said. "Here we are, fourth floor. We'll work our way down. This is a card for Mrs. Tosta. Her daughter sends a card every day. She's a sweet lady. She weighed two hundred and eighty pounds when she came here, right after we opened, and look at her now."

The woman seated before the window was still plump, but not fat. She was knitting an argyle sock in purple, blue, and green.

"Ah, my mail," she said cheerfully. "The best part of the day, except for when my doctor comes to see me. I'm going to ask him if I can't go home for the weekend, when he comes today. I think I'm well enough, don't you?"

"You'll have to ask and see," Sylvia told her, handing over the letter. "This is Mrs. Randall, Erin Randall. She's going to take my place when I leave."

"We're going to miss Sylvia," Mrs. Tosta said. "But I'm sure we're going to like you, too, Mrs. Randall."

It was that way for the next hour as they looked in on every patient. Many of them mentioned Dr. Brogan, almost always with respect and affection; even those who griped seemed to feel that he could be brought around to their way of thinking if they tried hard enough.

When they reached the main floor again, Sylvia led her back to the reception desk. "We have a new patient being admitted at about ten-thirty, so we'll go through that before we take our coffee break. A Mr. Denton. His daughter is married to Neal Lundstrom, you know, the head of San Cristobal Jewelers? They have a gorgeous house out by the Country Club. The old gentleman doesn't want to come—quite a few of them fight it, until they've been here for a short time—so don't be shocked if he's abusive. Some of them are that way."

The Lundstroms and Mr. Denton arrived on the dot of 10:30. Erin stood by, observing, after Sylvia had introduced her to them. Mrs. Lundstrom was clearly upset, her husband was a man accustomed to authority but somewhat out of his depth here, and Ernie Denton was livid.

"I don't need a goddamned wheelchair," he shouted as the ambulance attendants secured him in a collapsible chair. "Take me home, Paula! I want to go home!"

Mrs. Lundstrom dabbed at her eyes with a lace-edged hankie. "Daddy, I've explained to you why we have to bring you here. Please, just see what it's like."

Sylvia remained calm. "I'll have an aide take you to your room, Mr. Denton. Her name is Janet, and she'll take good care of you. After you're settled in, your daughter and your son-in-law can visit you, if you like. And then, after lunch, Dr. Brogan will welcome you himself. He always likes to make every new patient welcome."

"Dr. Brogan can kiss my ass!" the old man bellowed, so that heads turned among the patients reading or conversing or listening to music in the lounge. "Paula, you bitch, get me out of this place!"

Paula Lundstrom clutched at her husband's arm, and he drew her close, consolingly.

Sylvia gave them a kindly smile. "You can wait in the small lounge until he's settled in. It's the second door on the right, down the hall," she said. "Here's Janet. Take Mr. Denton to Room 204."

Janet was smiling too. "Let's go, Mr. Denton. You'll want to be all comfortable by the time they come around with lunch, won't you? I think there's veal scaloppine today."

"I don't want any of your goddamned scaloppine!" The massively obese old man struggled against the restraints that held him in the chair. His breathing was labored, his wheezing indicating even to the uninitiated, like Erin, that he had severe emphysema. He struck out at the aide, and the girl dodged him with the agility of long practice and swiveled the wheelchair away, toward the elevator.

Paula Lundstrom was crying openly now. Her husband was torn between compassion for her and frustrated fury with his father-in-law. "Maybe it would be best," he said through his teeth, "if we came back tomorrow. Maybe he'll have calmed down by then."

"Oh, no," Paula said quickly, pausing to blow her nose. "I promised him I'd see him today."

"This evening might be best," Sylvia suggested. "I assure you, he'll be feeling better by then."

"Do you think so?" It was obvious the woman wanted to believe it.

"Yes, I do. It's always difficult the first day. Visiting hours are from two to four, and seven to eight, though of course if there are special needs, you can visit at any time. Why don't you come back at seven?"

Paula nodded. "He didn't use to be this way," she told them earnestly. "It's only this last year—he's put on so much weight, and forgotten his table manners, and begun using obscene language—he never was that way before!"

Her husband touched her gently, leading her away.

Erin watched their receding backs thoughtfully. "Will he be calmer then?"

"Probably. Dr. Brogan doesn't use a lot of tranquilizers and sedatives for his patients, except maybe on the day they get here, if they're upset. He'll talk to the old man, and if he's still wild, he may prescribe something." She laughed ruefully. "I almost wish Doctor was more drug oriented. I'd ask him for a tranquilizer for myself. I feel as if I'm coming apart at the seams."

She looked down in surprise at the pencil that had snapped between her fingers. "Good grief! What's wrong with me? Come on, let's take our break."

Erin related it all to her mother-in-law that evening when she went to pick up Sammie.

"It's a magnificent old house. Built over forty years ago, and a little old-fashioned, but it's all been modernized. Everything in it is new, and it's not tile and Formica and sterility. It looks like a home. The staff has a separate dining room, and the food—you wouldn't believe the food! The same as the patients get, Sylvia said, and they have a fantastic cook. I can eat my main meal there, if I like; Sammie could have her toasted cheese sandwich and tomato soup oftener, I guess, as long as I keep up her vitamins. She doesn't like most meats, anyway."

Ted's mother smiled. "And you liked everybody."

"Yes. All the staff, anyway. I didn't meet Dr. Spaulding, I guess he works in a laboratory away from the main building, and doesn't have much to do with the patients directly. There's a business office staff of two, plus the head nurse and three shifts of nurses and aides. Two security men to a shift, several cleaning people, a male orderly on each shift, in case anybody needs to be strong-armed, Sylvia said. Like the old man who came in today, he fought everybody until Dr. Brogan talked to him. Nobody knows what he said, but Mr. Denton stopped yelling after that. And, of course, there's Dr. Brogan himself. Everybody says he's wonderful to work for."

"And a good salary, too. Oh, honey, I'm so glad for you," Ruth Randall said, sincerity on her plain, middle-aged face. "It's almost too good to be true, isn't it?"

"Almost," Erin agreed.

7.

The old man closed his eyes when he heard them coming. The corridors were heavily carpeted, but he heard their voices, murmuring. He closed his eyes and lay still, wishing his goddamned breathing wasn't so loud. If they really whispered, he *wouldn't* be able to hear them.

"I think he's asleep," Paula said from the doorway.

"Maybe we'd better not disturb him, then." Neal spoke just as softly.

"But I told him I'd visit him today. Darling, I can't break my word to him. He thinks I've abandoned him, and I have to make him understand that I haven't, that this is for his benefit as well as ours."

Neal made a grunting sound. "For our sanity, you mean. I'm sorry if it seemed like I pushed you into this, honey, but I couldn't bear the thought of eating another meal across the table from him, watching the spills and the crumbs going all over, watching him put food in his mouth with his fingers—Christ!"

"No, no, I don't blame you. I don't blame Daddy, either. He can't help it, Dr. Brogan says, it's not his fault, but we just couldn't *live* with it any longer."

"Look, let's go talk to the nurse, see what she says about him. We can check back later, and maybe he'll be awake."

"Dr. Brogan was still in his office when we passed it. Maybe we can talk to him," Paula suggested. "Did you ever hear of a more dedicated doctor? Still working this time of the evening?"

The voices receded, and Ernie Denton opened his eyes. It didn't look like a hospital room, he had to admit that. His hip still ached where they'd stuck that goddamned needle into it. The nurse had come into the room with the syringe on a tray, and that other doctor, the one whose name he'd forgotten already. Seedy sort of fellow, half-starved.

Ernie had glared suspiciously at the tray, at the pair of them. "What's that for?" he demanded.

"Dr. Brogan has ordered an injection for you. Remember, he told you about it?" The nurse had a low, husky voice that would have been soothing if she hadn't carried the tray with the needle. "This is Dr. Spaulding. He's going to give you the injection, Mr. Denton."

Spaulding, that was the doctor's name. Ernie felt a mild surge of triumph, that he'd remembered.

"What's it for?" he'd demanded.

"To make you feel better," the nurse told him. He remembered her name now, too. Miss Busby, only he thought of her as Miss Busty.

The skinny doctor didn't speak to him the entire time he was in the room. The nurse told him to roll over, and pushed down his pajama pants—at least they didn't make him put on one of those absurd gowns, but permitted his own pajamas, from home—and the doctor stuck the needle into his hip. It hurt like hell for about five minutes, and then the pain subsided to a dull ache that was there yet, hours later. He'd bet there was a bruise, too, but he couldn't twist around enough to see.

"There, that wasn't so bad, was it?" Miss Busby asked, and they went away and left him alone.

He'd been alone all day, except for when Dr. Brogan arrived after lunch. Cheerful, wearing a blue suit with a red and white silk tie, looking as if he'd just come from a beauty parlor. Ernie didn't trust men who had manicures and their hair marcelled.

"Good afternoon, Mr. Denton. Remember me? Dr. Brogan?"

The old man had stared at him sullenly. "What do you want me to do, kiss your goddamned ring?"

The doctor laughed. "Won't be necessary. Are you comfortable? Have a good lunch?"

It *had* been a good lunch, but he'd be goddamned if he'd admit it.

"It's boring in here," Ernie told him.

"Yes, well, you can watch television or listen to the radio, if you insist on staying in your room. Or you can join some of the others in the lounge, visit, get acquainted. Or one of the girls will take you out around the grounds, if you'd like some fresh air. It's a beautiful day, the leaves are all turning color and the fall flowers are still blooming, sunshine everywhere."

"I want my trains," Ernie told him.

"Ah, yes, your daughter mentioned that you'd recently bought $4,000 worth of trains." Brogan perched on the edge of the bed, swinging one foot.

"All to scale. Authentic models," Ernie told him. "I never had a train when I was a kid. Now I got trains, and they won't let me use them."

"Take up a lot of space, do they?" Brogan seemed genuinely interested.

"Half the basement, at my son-in-law's house. *My* house."

"Couldn't put them up in here, then. Maybe we could find space for them in our basement, though. I'll have a look. There's an elevator goes from this floor down there, easy enough to get to. It would probably take a little remodeling. I'll speak to your daughter about it."

Ernie stared at him. Was this guy on the level? Before he figured it out, the doctor changed the subject.

"One of the reasons you're here, Mr. Denton, is that you're obese. You know that, don't you?"

"Over three hundred pounds," Ernie said. There was satisfaction in his voice.

"Yes. Well, I think you need to lose about a hundred and twenty-five to a hundred and fifty pounds of that."

Ernie stared at the man, appalled. Was that what they'd brought him here for, to be starved to death? "I'm eighty-two years old, for crissake. What difference does it make now?"

"The weight is going to kill you, you know. It's working on killing you right now. Those extra pounds are hard on your heart, your lungs, all your organs. They're all working overtime, because of that fat."

Ernie swore, words he'd never said aloud in front of anybody until the last year or so. "Everybody's going to die of something, aren't they? So what difference does it make if it's from being too fat? I like to eat. It's the only goddamned thing left I can do that I enjoy, except run the trains."

Brogan nodded. "We all enjoy eating. What do you like best?"

The old man stared at him defiantly. "Pork chops."

The doctor said nothing about cholesterol or calories, only nodding again. "What else?"

"Hot biscuits with butter and honey. Fried eggs, with ham. Strawberry shortcake with whipped cream. Chocolate cake."

"Uh-huh," Brogan said. "What about salads? Raw vegetables?"

Ernie's heart sank. "You got false teeth?" he asked. "You ever try to chew carrots and celery with false teeth?"

"How about gazpacho? You like that?"

"What the hell's gazpacho?"

"It's a sort of thick soup, served cold, of puréed vegetables. Cucumbers, tomatoes, onions, avocado."

Ernie's voice rose in disbelief. "Cold soup?"

"It's delicious. Tell me, can you write legibly?"

Ernie was so furious he refused to reply.

"If you can make us a list of your favorite foods—include the pork chops and the chocolate cake—we'll work up a diet for you. You can keep some of your favorites, and try some of our stuff, fair enough? If you can't write it out, one of the girls will bring you a list, and you can check things off on it. Maybe that would be easiest." Brogan stood up. "Anything you need or want, let me know."

Ernie was too confused to answer, and Brogan didn't seem to care, one way or the other.

Dinner had been excellent. He'd looked over the tray, scowling at the little bowl of soup. No steam rising from it. The aide, Janet, smiled at him.

"Doctor says if you eat the gazpacho, you can have cake for dessert. It's the honor system, I've brought it all, and we'll trust you to eat everything on your tray before the cake. Of course, if you cheat or refuse anything, then we won't bring dessert next time. Fair enough?"

He was getting sick of that phrase. What was fair about being hauled off to a rest home to die?

On the other hand, the rare roast beef with its side dish of horseradish, the baked potato, the bright green broccoli, didn't look all that bad. And the cake. Chocolate, layered, with chocolate frosting. It was only that goddamned cold soup.

He supposed he could pour it down the toilet. Only he wouldn't put it past them to have a hidden camera somewhere.

He ate everything on the main plate, and nibbled on the cake. Good. Very good. But there was still the cold soup.

He supposed he'd have to gag it down. They had him between a rock and a hard place, and he didn't want them to cut him off and bring him *just* cold soup. He picked up the spoon and took a cautious taste.

To his astonishment, it was delicious. He scraped out the bowl, then devoured the cake, ignoring the fork and using his fingers. The crumbs went down the front of his pajamas and spilled onto the sheets, unnoticed.

He wondered if they'd bring him a snack before it was time to go to sleep.

8.

On Wednesday Erin found Sylvia weeping in the rest room.

It had a small, outer lounge, with a couch and several comfortable chairs besides the two that faced the dressing table against the mirrored wall. Sylvia sat there, hunched over the vanity, her shoulders shaking.

Erin stopped, and would have withdrawn to save the other girl embarrassment, but Sylvia lifted her head and they stared at one another in the mirror.

"I'm sorry, I'm intruding—Sylvia, what is it? Is there anything I can do?"

Sylvia mopped at her wet face with a handful of Kleenex. She drew a long, hiccuping breath. "No, nothing. Just cover for me, if Dr. Brogan comes around. He'll be bound to want to know what's the matter."

Erin closed the outer door and drew closer. "What *is* the matter? Do you want to talk about it?"

"I feel so stupid. Sometimes I wonder if I'm going crazy."

Erin sank onto the other chair beside her. "Of course you aren't going crazy. Are you ill? Or is it just the pressure of getting ready for your wedding?"

"I didn't sleep last night. I mean literally, hardly at all. So I'm tired, and there's so much to be done, and this morning on the way to work—Zack drove me, because we decided to sell my car, and my neighbor took it to try it out—we had the most terrible fight."

Erin reached out a hand to cover the one with the engagement ring on it. "You were out of sorts because you hadn't rested properly. He'll understand that, won't he? Lovers' quarrels can be made up, you know."

"I don't even know if I want to marry him anymore," Sylvia said.

"Oh, honey, of course you do! You've been telling me how much you love him, and he loves you. Just because you've disagreed on something doesn't mean you have to call it all off. Chances are when he picks you up tonight, he'll apologize. Or you apologize, and kiss and make up."

"I don't know. I don't know what's the matter with me. I never thought Zack would speak to me that way, or that I'd scream back at him. It was horrible."

"You wait and see. By this afternoon you'll be able to make it up," Erin told her, hoping she was right. "Do you want me to go ahead and take the mail around by myself?"

Sylvia's voice was muffled. "Yes. Why don't you do that? I'm going to put a cold cloth on my eyes before anyone else sees me. Maybe they'll just think I've cried because I'm sorry to be leaving."

"Sure," Erin agreed, and left her there.

She was too enthusiastic about what she was doing to dwell for long on Sylvia's nerves, or whatever it was. After she'd delivered the mail, learning a little about each of the patients as she went, she spent half an hour in the business office, set up in what had once been a den. The two young women who worked there, Lois Nelson and Evelyn McKay, were attractive, smartly dressed, briskly efficient, and busy; nevertheless, they took time to make her feel at home.

They didn't use typewriters. Each worked with a computer keyboard attached to a TV screen; the work was printed out by a separate piece of machinery at something in excess of six hundred words per minute, error-free. They were proud of having the latest in electronic equipment, and happy to talk about it.

"I'm taking a night class in computers," Erin told them. "It's fascinating, isn't it?"

They explained to her a little of what they did, mostly handling the billing for the patients and accepting the checks that came in, plus the payroll and routine hospital records. Evelyn did the accounting, Lois typed up patient records from Dr. Brogan's dictation, and everything ran smoothly and efficiently.

"If there's ever any need for more help here," Erin offered, "I'd be happy to step in. I want to use what I'm learning at school."

"We'll think about that, come vacation time," Evelyn assured her, and Erin went back to the reception desk.

The following morning when Erin arrived, Sylvia was not at the desk. Neither was she in the rest room, which Erin cautiously checked, so Erin went on with the work she was familiar with. At five minutes to ten, Vonda Busby burst into Dr. Brogan's office as Erin was depositing a stack of letters on his desk, being careful to avoid the vase and the bronze chrysanthemum she had placed there earlier.

Vonda had not knocked, and when they turned to face her there was no mistaking her agitation. "Have you heard about Sylvia?" she asked. "It just came over the radio. They heard it in the kitchen."

Erin froze, and Matt Brogan came up out of his executive's chair.

"What about Sylvia?" he asked. "What's happened?"

"She's dead," Vonda Busby said. "Sylvia's dead. They said she committed suicide."

Erin rested a hand on the edge of the desk for support, and saw her own shock mirrored on Dr. Brogan's face.

"Sylvia? Are they sure? For God's sake, the girl was happy as a clam, she was getting married in a week or so . . . Suicide?" He was incredulous.

"I thought you'd want to . . . to confirm it," Vonda said. Her lipstick was too bright against pale skin.

"Yes. Yes, of course. I can't believe it. She was so *happy*, she was looking forward to . . ." He pulled himself together and turned toward Erin. "Well, you didn't know her as well as we did, of course, but I'm sure this is upsetting to you, too. You've been with her almost constantly for the past few days; did she say anything to indicate she was in a suicidal state of mind?"

"She was upset yesterday when she came in because she'd had an argument with her boyfriend. But I certainly didn't think it was anything serious," Erin said slowly.

"Well, listen, both of you, not a word to the patients, not until we have more particulars. I suppose there's no way to prevent them hearing it on the radio, but if we can keep it quiet until we know the facts . . . Erin"—by the second day he had begun to call her by her first name, the way he did with all the others—"I'm sorry, this may make it a little more difficult for you, but carry on as best you can. If there are any phone calls, from the newspapers or anything like that, simply say that we have no comment on the matter, that we've only just heard of it ourselves."

"Yes, of course," Erin said. She left the two of them talking, forgetting that she had several more letters to deliver.

Greatly subdued, and with a sense of loss of one who was beginning to be a friend, Erin sat at the small desk and wondered what she might have done to have prevented such a tragedy.

It must have been a slow day for news, for they ran her picture on the fourth page of the *Record*. Silas Copetti skimmed through the newspaper while he ate his solitary supper of bacon and eggs and English muffins and frozen hash-browns. It was his favorite breakfast, but he never had time to make it in the morning. He was washing it down with a can of beer when he saw the picture and paused.

"SUICIDE," it said. The face was vaguely familiar, and for a minute he couldn't figure out why. A round-faced, chubby, shy-looking young girl with fair hair, quite undistinguished.

He read the accompanying story, thinking she'd probably ridden in the cab at some time, or maybe he'd even arrested her for shoplifting or something, once.

Sylvia Miller, 28, was found dead in her bathroom at 1753 Edmonds Street last night by her fiancé, Zack Vladika, when he and a friend broke down the door to reach her. She had apparently hanged herself from a light fixture. Vladika said he knew of no reason why she should have committed suicide, as they were to have been married within the month. Police spokesmen said that no further investigation is anticipated. Miss Miller was employed by a local hospital as a receptionist. She is survived by her parents, Henry and Gladys Miller, and two brothers, Alan and Karl, of this city.

Two key words reached out and grabbed Silas. *Hospital* and *Zack*.

Christ, could it be the same girl? The one he'd picked up at Forest Hills?

He tilted the paper under the lamp to see it better. Yes, there was a similarity in the mouth and eyes, but God, how could it be the same girl? The one he'd taken to a dental appointment had been so skinny her clothes were falling off her. This one was positively fat.

It said this Sylvia Miller had worked at a hospital, and her fiancé's name was Zack. It had to be the same one.

Suicide. He picked up the last strip of bacon in his fingers and thoughtfully bit it in half. The fiancé didn't know any reason why she'd have wanted to kill herself; they were planning to be married. That matched with what Silas remembered. The young woman had been happy, looking forward to her wedding, and to quitting her job at the hospital, although she liked the job.

There was nothing to go on, really. People killed themselves every day, over the stupidest damned things. Silas knew, because he'd seen a lot of them. They'd failed a test, or lost a job, or a lover, or had their car repossessed. One he recalled had attempted suicide by drinking Drāno because his wife had told him she was leaving him.

So maybe something happened to this Sylvia Miller that made her go from happy bride to suicide. If she hadn't worked at the hospital where Uncle Isadore had died, he'd never have given the matter another thought.

Hell, people died all the time. There would naturally be a higher than average mortality rate among inmates in a rest home; they were sick when they went there, their families expected them to die. Yet Sylvia Miller was young; she certainly hadn't seemed ill a week ago, and she hadn't sounded like someone who'd kill herself, either.

Aunt Tillie hadn't been able to say what she thought was fishy about Isadore's death. And Silas couldn't have said why he was bothered now. But he was.

He put the paper aside and reached for the phone book, consulting the article before he flipped the pages. Vladika, shouldn't be too many of those, he thought, and found it. Zachary Vladika.

The address was less than two miles away. Silas picked up the phone, then dropped it back into its cradle. A P.I. who took on cases that were none of his business, with nobody to pick up the tab for the expense account, was a fool. Yet that little prickling uneasiness that he'd felt about Uncle Isadore was there again, and he felt compelled to follow up on it.

He dropped his dishes in the sink and locked the door behind him on the way out.

There was a KBLA van parked on the street, and more cars than were probably customary. Silas parked in front of a house that was dark and walked across the street and up onto the porch of the old white frame house.

Every light in the place was on, and he had to step over a cable from the TV van. He'd been thinking out his approach on this one, and now he didn't have to use it, because the front door was wide open and there were so many people milling around that nobody paid any attention to him.

The Vladikas sat facing the TV camera crew on a brown couch. It was easy to identify them, even if the newsman hadn't called them by name.

The young fellow in the middle was undoubtedly Zack. He sat with his elbows on his knees, sunken into the couch, and his eyes were red. The stocky couple flanking him were his parents, and the boy perched on the arm of the couch was a younger brother.

Silas was surprised that the ghouls were here for a simple suicide, when the victim wasn't a prominent person. But if there wasn't much else in the way of news, and they had half an hour to fill on the screen at eleven, maybe this was the most exciting thing they could come up with.

He'd arrived at exactly the right moment. The crew was just getting under way. One of them held a photograph before the camera, and when he put it aside to focus on the shocked and grieving family Silas stepped over and took a look.

Yes, it was the same girl, the one he'd carried in the cab. Only in this picture she was about halfway between the fat girl in the newspaper photo and the skinny one he remembered.

He stood to one side, amid other onlookers who were either neighbors or relatives of Sylvia's fiancé and listened while Zachary Vladika spoke for the benefit of KBLA's watchers. He was dark, husky, with a prominent Adam's apple that bobbed with emotion even when he wasn't speaking.

"We were going to be married, week from Saturday," he said. "I drove her to work yesterday morning, and we had a little argument. Nothing serious, at least I didn't think so. She seemed okay when I picked her up last night and brought her home, except she didn't say much. She said she was going to stay home and wash her hair last night, didn't want me to come over. So I didn't, until this morning, when it was time to take her to work again."

He gulped air, and the Adam's apple ran up and down like a yo-yo.

"Tell us what happened when you got to her house," the ghoul asked. Silas knew him; his name was Earl Whippler, and he had a practiced, syrupy tone for occasions such as this, when he wanted to pump the relatives or the witnesses to some gory event.

Zack's tears were visible from across the room. "She didn't come out, so I went up to the door and knocked. And then when she didn't answer, I unlocked the door and went in. I got a key, I've been packing stuff for her to move out—anyway, I couldn't find her, only the bathroom door was locked. When she didn't answer, I got Gene—my buddy, I take him to work too—and we busted in the door. And found her."

His face crumpled, and the camera zoomed in closer; Silas knew that because he'd watched KBLA news before, and they always gave you a close-up at a time like this.

It took the man a minute to regain control. "She—she was hanging from the light fixture in the bathroom ceiling. It had come partway down, but not enough so her feet touched anything. She had a—a belt around her neck. A blue belt. I was going to climb on the edge of the tub and cut her down, but Gene said"—he gulped again—"she was dead. She was cold, we couldn't help her, she must of done it last night. Gene said we better call the police. So we did."

A tall gangling young man—Gene?—stepped forward from a corner where he'd been standing. He cleared his throat. "The cops said it was a clear case of suicide. I mean, the window in there was a little bitty one and painted shut, hadn't been opened in years. And the door was locked. She had to have done it herself."

"Did she leave a note? Make a phone call to anyone, before she did it?" Earl Whippler asked gently.

"No," Zack and Gene said at the same time.

The interview was over. No more than two minutes on the late news, probably. The camera crew began to coil up their cables.

The woman beside Zack got up, moving heavily. "I'll get some coffee if anybody wants it."

Apparently most of them did, except the KBLA crew. Silas stepped to one side to let them out the front door. There was general milling around, and Silas wound up next to Zack, holding a steaming cup that read *Damn, I'm good.*

"Mr. Vladika," he said, under cover of half a dozen simultaneous conversations. "My name's Copetti." He flashed his identification, confident that the guy wouldn't know the difference, cop from private investigator. Nobody ever really looked at the ID that was offered.

Zack stared at him dully. "You didn't find anything more, did you?"

"Just wanted to ask a few more questions, if it's not too much trouble."

Zack wiped the back of his hand across his nose. "Sure."

"This quarrel you had with Miss Miller, yesterday morning. Could you tell me what it was about?"

His buddy, Gene, spoke sharply. "I thought the case was closed. It was suicide, so what difference does it make?"

Silas gave him a level look. "We like to have reasons, know why things happen. Were you there, sir, when the quarrel took place?"

If the guy refused to answer, there was nothing Silas could do about it. Yet after a momentary hesitation, Gene surrendered to the authoritative note, as most people usually did.

"Yeah, I was there. I ride to work with Zack all the time. It wasn't much of a fight. Nothing anybody in her right mind would kill herself over."

"Did it have anything to do with the hospital where she worked?"

Zack scowled. "Why would it have anything to do with the hospital? She was quitting there, she gave notice."

Gene kept his voice low, but he sounded angry. "What are you trying to do? Make him feel guilty because he had a few words with the girl and she killed herself? Nothing Zack said was bad enough to make her do that."

"Maybe not. So if it wasn't important, what's the big secret? They had the fight, or whatever it was, in front of you, so it couldn't have been all that personal."

"Oh, hell," Zack said suddenly, savagely. "He's right. I'll admit she'd been awfully nervous lately. I never thought it would make her cry when I mentioned her weight, but she wouldn't kill herself over that, would she?"

"What about her weight?" Silas probed in a quiet voice. "She was nice and slim."

"Yeah, but when I first met her," Zack said, sipping at his own coffee, "she was kinda heavy. I didn't see how pretty she was until she lost another twenty pounds or so. Only she kept on losing, and I told her it was time to stop. I told her I like a little meat on my women, I didn't want to go to bed with a skeleton. That was all. She wouldn't have hung herself over that, would she?"

His dark eyes pleaded for assurance, and Silas gave it to him. "I wouldn't think so. She was pretty sensible, wasn't she?"

Zack slumped back on the couch. "Yeah, I thought so. I don't understand. I don't think it was anything I did, but I can't think of anything else, either."

"She didn't have problems on the job, did she?"

"She loved the job. Sometimes I even felt jealous of that doctor she worked for. Not that there was anything between them, I don't mean that. But she admired him a lot."

"St. Brogan," Silas muttered, and Zack nodded.

"Yeah, kind of like that. He never said or did anything wrong, and that ain't natural."

Driving home, Silas echoed Zack's final phrase. It wasn't natural for anybody to be as perfect as Matthew Brogan, M.D. Maybe that was what kept sticking in his craw, in the face of a complete lack of evidence that anything peculiar was going on at Forest Hills.

It just sure as hell wasn't natural.

9.

Joan Warlum, R.N., was within twenty minutes of the end of her working day. She still had several charts to complete, and she sighed. Doug was going to be annoyed if she was late again tonight, but what could she do about it? A nurse couldn't always quit just because the whistle blew.

She reached for the next chart on the stack, flipped through the pages, and cursed softly under her breath. Mr. Denton hadn't had his injection yet, though it had been scheduled for half an hour ago.

She looked around and saw only an aide, who was not qualified to give injections. Joan sighed, stood, and pulled out her key for the medicine room.

She filled the syringe from the small bottle enigmatically labeled *A.S.* and placed it on her tray, hoping that by some miracle Ernie Denton would be in a better mood than when she had injected him yesterday.

She found him watching television, and put on her best professional smile. "Time for medication," she said cheerfully.

The old man was so fat it was obscene. There were traces of gravy from lunch on the front of his blue pajamas. Joan made a mental note to speak to Janet about that; what if his family came to visit and found him in soiled garments? She put the tray down on the bedside table. "Roll over for me, please," she said. "On your left side."

To her relief he obeyed, though he growled back at her. "Am I going to have to have one of these goddamned shots every day?"

"If Doctor orders it," Joan said calmly. She jerked down the trousers and slapped the massive hip sharply, then drove the needle in before he could yelp. "There, all done."

He grimaced, rolling once more onto his back. "Hurts like hell.

Like to see how *he'd* like it, if somebody stuck that thing in his butt every day. Bet he'd find some way to get it in pill form."

He began to cough, and she brought him a glass of water, waiting until he'd gotten the spasm under control before she left the room. Much easier than she'd expected; perhaps he was coming around, she thought.

"Mrs. Warlum!" It was Janet, at the far end of the corridor. "Come quick, Mrs. Hampton's having some kind of seizure!"

Joan hit the button to summon assistance, and for the next quarter of an hour she and Vonda Busby and Dr. Brogan worked over the elderly woman.

"There, I think she's stabilized," Vonda said at last. "Janet, you'd better stay with her for a while. Get the vitals every quarter of an hour. If her blood pressure fluctuates more than ten points, call me."

Dr. Brogan exhaled as he stepped away from the bed, loosening his tie. "I'll be in my office, if there's any further difficulty," he said.

Vonda glanced at her watch, then spoke to the other R.N. "You're on overtime, Joan. Go ahead, take off."

"Thanks. See you tomorrow, then." Joan took her leave, and the other two walked more slowly along the corridor.

"I understand you talked Mr. Denton's daughter into paying for fixing up the basement for the old man's trains," Vonda said. "What's it costing her?"

"Fifty-five hundred dollars." Brogan looked down into her laughing face. "Well, it's hardly customary medical expense. And she can afford it."

"And when he's gone, there will be a modern, attractive rec room in the basement."

He nodded complacently, and her chuckle was audible.

The P.M. shift nurses were just coming on, talking and laughing in the staff rest room behind the nurses' station. Vonda slid into her seat, reaching for the charts that she would have to review with the next shift before her own was ended, then realizing that one chart lay open.

There was the order for Mr. Denton's injection, and no notation that he'd received it. No doubt at about the time Joan would have given it, Mrs. Hampton had gone sour, and Joan had forgotten it.

Vonda rose at once, unlocked the medicine room, and filled the syringe. When she entered Room 204, the old man glared at her and held the covers down with both hands.

"What the hell's that? Another shot? For crissake, they think I'm a pin cushion or what?"

"Roll over, please. On your left side. Did they tell you that the workmen are coming tomorrow, to turn the basement into a room where you can run your trains?"

"They are? Who's paying for it?"

"Your daughter and son-in-law." She jerked down his pajama pants. "You're lucky to have relatives who care about you."

He made a snorting noise, then howled when the needle sank in. "God, it hurts worse every time! They don't care about me, they just want me out of their house. *My* house! They even took my name off the goddamned mailbox, did you know that? They said it would be best if I signed it over to them, save on taxes or some such."

She nodded her blond head. "That's often done these days. There's no point in anyone paying taxes they don't have to pay. Would you like to get up for dinner tonight? Eat in the dining room?"

She didn't flinch at the profanity he flung at her, only gave him a cool smile and closed the door as she let herself out. What an old bastard he was, she thought. Well, Dr. Brogan will smooth off the rough edges if anyone can. And when they got that fat off him, he'd at least look better, even if he continued to sound like an obscene phone call.

She went back to her station and entered the injection on his chart, then turned to face the oncoming shift.

Half a dozen times a day, without consciously planning it, Silas found himself driving past Forest Hills.

It was easy to tell when it was visiting hours. The parking area would be full of expensive cars. It wasn't a place for poor people, that was for damned sure. He'd checked with his cousins to see just how much the "small" loan against Tillie's house had been, and felt sick when he found out. So much, for such a brief period of time. Yet Tillie felt it was worth it, except that the old man had died there.

Once he had a fare whose own chauffeur was ill, so she'd called a cab to go and see her mother at Forest Hills.

He let her out directly in front of the main entrance, and through the double glass doors he saw the redhead, the one with the terrific legs, talking to a couple who'd arrived just ahead of his fare. She wore green, and she was, as he remembered, stunning.

He didn't learn the name of his passenger, but he did extract a fair amount of information. Her mother was ninety-three, had been a patient at Forest Hills since the place opened, and though she'd wept at the idea of being put into a home, she had been perfectly satisfied once she'd gotten accustomed to it.

"I hear it's a nice place," Silas said, and that was enough to set the woman off.

"Oh, yes, it's marvelous. They're so good to the patients, you don't have to feel guilty about your mother being there. Everyone is so kind. The food is superb. And Dr. Brogan is so interested."

St. Brogan again, Si thought. It gave him no reassurance, however.

He supposed it was possible that Matthew Brogan really was what he seemed. A conscientious and caring doctor who had been lucky enough to inherit money from a grateful patient, enabling him to turn the estate into just the kind of rest home everybody would like to see.

It ate at Silas like a small cancer, not too painful yet, able to be forgotten for long periods of time, yet gnawing away steadily, resurfacing at odd moments. It didn't feel right. He didn't believe in perfection.

He took Patty to the zoo on Sunday afternoon, forgot everything else in the pleasure—not unmingled with pain—of having his small daughter with him for the day. She clung to his hand and skipped along beside him, chattering incessantly in the way that Diana said drove her crazy. Patty had his coloring, dark hair and gray eyes, and she was tanned after a summer in the sun. She conned him into hot dogs and Pepsi and ice cream, not what her mother would have approved for dinner, but what the hell? They didn't do it very often, and he wanted Patty to remember the day with pleasure. They had so little time together now.

It wasn't that Diana was unreasonable about visitation rights, but he had so few free hours when a seven-year-old was awake. By the time he wound up his day with the cab, she'd already been put to bed. On weekends, some of which he worked, Patty's days were full too. And there were excursions with her mother: "Si, I really have to get her some shoes, and everything she has is too short. We *have* to spend Saturday shopping, we really do."

When he took her home, to the house where he'd once lived, which held both sweet and bitter memories, the child had hugged him tightly and kissed him good-bye. "I had a good time, Daddy. Can we go again next week?"

"Probably not," he told her gently. "I think your mama has other plans. But maybe Sunday after next we could take a lunch and go to the park, if the weather's nice. How about that?"

"Okay," Patty agreed, and trotted up the sidewalk to the doorway, where Diana was waiting for her.

He'd completed the case he'd been working on, just a matter of a lot of phone calls and then a trip upstate to look at some photos. He'd found the client's daughter, and it was both better and worse than the previous missing-child case.

This one hadn't been a hooker or a drug addict, but she'd been dead. Hitchhiking, they said, and she'd been hit by a car and had bled to death beside the road.

The client handed over his check, wiping at his eyes. "Well, at least we know, Mr. Copetti. That was what was killing us, imagining. . . . Now we know."

There was a message on his answering machine when he got home that night. "Hi, Si, this is Grady. Thought you might be interested to know that Mitchum is having problems. The guys are betting, four to one, that he's on a slide. Maybe all the way."

Well. Silas played the message again, feeling a minor uplift. Mitchum was a captain on the San Cristobal P.D. and directly responsible for the fact that Silas Copetti was no longer a sergeant. The bastard had perjured himself before, leaving Si hanging in midair, with nothing to grab onto; maybe he'd repeated the performance, only this time he got caught in his own trap. Let him slide, all the way to the gutter, which was where the son of a bitch belonged.

His longing to be part of that elite fraternity again was an ache that couldn't be assuaged by anything. Not alcohol, not a woman, not anything. He'd gotten his license to do private investigating because he had the necessary skills to do it, but it wasn't the same as being a cop. Much of the time he felt tainted, soiled, by what he did as a P.I. Sneaking around watching husbands or wives who were cheating. He knew there were decent people left in the world, but it was hard to remember that when he saw so many of the other kind. It bothered him more than dealing with drunks, thieves, prostitutes, and murderers.

He missed being married, too. He and Diana had had some good years, before the bad times came. She'd never liked being married to a cop, though; she'd never understood how he felt about that. She'd hated it when he didn't come home on time, and it didn't matter whether he called to tell her he'd be late or not. She didn't want to hear what he'd been involved in, and he didn't really want to tell her, but he'd had to tell somebody. You couldn't handle a head-on crash that killed six people, including two little kids, and help load the victims into ambulances and hose the blood off the street and just go home and say, "Hi, honey, what's for supper?"

You had to gather with your peers, like the cops in that book Waumbaugh wrote, *The Choir Boys,* and talk it out. Let some of the tension drain away, so that when you closed your eyes you didn't see a child's severed hand lying against the curb. And while you talked to other men who'd seen the same things, who knew what shape your guts were in, you had a few beers. He'd never been one to overdo that, the drinking. Lots of cops became alcoholics, but he'd determined he never would. Only two beers smelled the same as the brewery, and Diana would draw back from him with distaste, and make some remark that would cause his temper to flare.

The marriage had gone down the tubes, and he supposed it was better for Patty not to live with two parents who were always snarling at each other, yet he missed the good parts so damned much. The barbecues in the backyard, the romps on the beach, the quiet evenings reading or watching TV. Except that toward the end even TV had become a battleground. He was fascinated by "Hill Street Blues" and "St. Elsewhere," both of which seemed to him realistic and worthwhile. Diana couldn't bear either one.

"For God's sake, isn't it enough that you're up to your ears in blood and gore all day, and then you have to watch more of it at night?"

So now he could watch whatever he liked, and eat whatever he liked, and nobody cared how many beers he had. Only there was no camaraderie in his life anymore. Not that the guys weren't friendly, if he dropped in at Smitty's. They'd make room for him at a table or a booth, and ask how things were going, and drink with him.

But he wasn't part of the fraternity anymore. He was an outsider. He didn't know what was happening in department politics, he didn't understand the inside jokes unless they explained them to him, and that made it even more clear that he was an outsider.

He was in limbo, Silas thought. He lived, after a fashion. He fixed his solitary meals. He read the paper and went to bed, alone. Oh, there'd been a few women, right after he and Diana split, but he'd had the real thing, once. One-night stands might be okay to brag about to your buddies, but they weren't worth a shit in the long run.

Hell, he was only thirty-eight. That wasn't too old to start over, even to have more kids, though no other kid would ever mean as much to him as Patty. Why wouldn't he still have a chance at happiness?

He didn't know why, but that made him think about the redhead with the gorgeous legs. He knew her name, and her address. Erin Randall. Eleven-twenty Fir Street, Apartment Four. But she had a husband, according to the car registration. He wondered if she was happy.

And then, on Saturday morning, he ran into her, the redhead. Literally.

10.

Matthew Brogan took off the glasses he used for close work, pinched the bridge of his nose, and sighed heavily. It had been a long day. He pushed the stack of charts to one side, turned off the dictating equipment, and put the spool of tape on top of the charts. When Lois arrived in the morning she would pick up the charts and tapes, and transcribe what he had dictated onto the computer, which would then be printed out for permanent insertion into the charts.

He stacked the dishes neatly on the tray he'd brought from the kitchen. He seldom ate at his desk; tonight had been an exception. There had simply been so much to do. It was gratifying that the hospital was nearly at capacity—at their present rate of patient acceptance they would, within a month or two, have to set up a waiting list.

This aroused considerable gratification. The reputation of Forest Hills—of Matthew Brogan, M.D.—had grown substantially since he'd opened the hospital eight months earlier. They were even getting inquiries, and a few patients, from out-of-state.

He sat for a moment, considering the question of hiring another doctor soon. He needed the help, if he were not to spend more and more evenings in his office catching up on the dictation he hadn't found time to do during the day. Evenings when he might otherwise have been having dinner with an attractive young woman, like Vonda Busby. Remembering their last such evening, two nights ago, brought a smile to his lips. He'd made it clear he wasn't going to offer marriage, though he was sure that was what she'd initially intended, but she'd let him kiss her in a very satisfactory manner; he wondered if buying her a little gift might not weaken her resolve to hold out against the obviously mutual attraction.

There was an office already furnished for an assistant; he had foreseen the necessity for one, though he hadn't really thought it would come this soon. So there was only the matter of choosing the right man—or perhaps woman—and the question of salary.

Yes, a young woman, he thought, forgetting momentarily how weary he was. How did you find a woman, when you couldn't very well advertise that that was what you wanted? Oh, nonsense, all he had to do was let the word get around among his colleagues that he'd be willing to *consider* a female, and they'd apply. A bright, pretty young thing, yes. Not one who would in any way interfere with his own ideas of treatment, just a nice, intelligent girl, preferably unmarried. Things could get so messy when the girl was married.

To attract the kind of doctor he wanted, he'd have to pay a fairly substantial salary, though if he got one right out of school he might get by for a year or so on less. He wanted to be able to offer a sum that would be attractive to an M.D. looking for a position and sufficient to hold her. A turnover in employees was not only a nuisance, it was expensive. Even with the little people, like Sylvia Miller, though he had to admit that Erin Randall was a worthy replacement and was learning very quickly.

He got sidetracked for a minute, thinking about Sylvia. God, she was one of his successes, though of course he hadn't been able to tell anyone about it. A thoroughly nice girl. He couldn't imagine why she would have done something so stupid as to hang herself. But then, there was no understanding people, especially females.

Brogan stood up and aligned the charts neatly at the corner of the desk, then picked up his dishes to carry them back to the kitchen.

The corridors were dimly lighted, empty. Somewhere someone was listening to music; from another quarter came canned laughter on TV. He moved silently along the corridor, nodding at Fran Barker, the night nurse, as she came out of the elevator.

"Everything all right?" he asked, and she gave him a smile.

"Just fine, Doctor. I've given Mr. Denton a sedative. He was rather abusive earlier—he upset Karen so she was nearly in tears. He's asleep now."

"How's Mrs. Hampton?"

"Quiet and stable."

"Good. Carry on," he said, and went on through the swinging doors into the huge kitchen.

It was as modern and well-equipped as any superior restaurant. Stainless steel, spotless counters and floors, the quiet hum of refrigerators and freezers. He left his dishes on the tray beside the sink, then opened the nearest refrigerator to see what there might be for a small snack. He wasn't much of a snacker—he'd never had to watch what he ate, but it was a habit of long-standing. (He was well aware of how big a part his own appearance played in dealing with relatives of patients, and even with patients themselves.) The habit held. There were green apples in a bin, his favorite Granny Smiths, and he took one, carefully washing it before he bit into the crisp flesh.

Usually he went out the other door, but since that would mean retracing his steps, Brogan let himself out onto the rear service area. He had taken no more than three steps on the asphalt when a broad beam of light hit him at mid-chest, rose to his face, then quickly was lowered to the ground.

"Evening, Doctor."

"Good evening, Steiner. Everything quiet?"

"All quiet, sir."

"Good." Across the lawn he could see lights in the laboratory. "Dr. Spaulding still working?"

"Yes, sir. He's still there. Puts in very long hours, doesn't he, sir?"

"Yes. Forgets to look at the clock sometimes. Think I'll go remind him that it's past ten. Good night, Steiner."

"Good night, Doctor."

Brogan stayed on the paved path this time, because the grass was undoubtedly wet and he was wearing a pair of his favorite suede shoes. He pushed open the door and looked at the hunched figure at the desk.

"Aaron, you know what time it is?"

"Ummm? Oh, Matt." Aaron Spaulding rubbed at the back of his neck, but as if he didn't really realize that it ached. "Just working out some statistics."

Brogan suppressed a mild irritation. "Why don't you let me get you that computer we talked about, and you could do in minutes what now takes you hours, all that figuring in your head."

"No, no. I can think better this way. I'd only be intimidated by a computer." Spaulding waved a vague hand. "Sit down, I'll have this in a few more minutes."

"Did you have any dinner?"

Spaulding blinked in the light when he lifted his head. "Dinner?"

"For God's sake, how do you expect your mind to work efficiently when you don't give it any fuel? Come on, it's well past quitting time. Let's go home and get some sleep. This will still be here in the morning; it doesn't matter whether you complete it tonight or not."

Spaulding was used to Brogan's impatience, and impervious to it. "Sometimes I think I'm so close. So *close*, Matt! The figures work out, the patient statistics seem to indicate that I'm gaining on it. Sometimes I feel there's something here that's all wrong; if I could just see what it is, it would be the last step. I know we're getting good results, we're prolonging lives, but we don't have a cure yet. And damm it, I want that cure! I don't want anyone else to die the way that Lisa did."

Brogan's voice softened. "Lisa wouldn't have let you work all night without eating. Come on, close up shop, go home."

Spaulding's smile was as wry as it was tired. "Once that phrase meant something. I had a home to go to, a wife to go to. It doesn't really matter anymore."

"How can you say that? It matters that you finish your work, doesn't it? You're a bloody genius. You've saved lives, and you'll save more. But you can't make your body run on sheer nervous energy. You have to have food, and you have to have rest." Brogan reached over and turned off the light that had been focused on the papers on the desk, leaving only a small light burning near the rat cages at the far end of the room. "Let's go. Get your key and lock up."

Spaulding rose somewhat stiffly and grinned. Then, for only a moment, Brogan glimpsed what his sister must have seen in the man. "I think I'm getting arthritic. Maybe I should turn to researching arthritis, when I've conquered cancer, eh?"

"Ought to be worthwhile," Brogan admitted, pausing while the other man secured the door behind them. They walked toward the condo together, not talking. Brogan was wondering if Vonda was still up, if she'd share a drink with him. Sometimes, after a hard day, a drink could be relaxing. Like everything else, alcohol could be a blessing when used in moderation. That was the key, he thought, moderation in all things.

11.

Silas caught the phone on the fifth ring. "Yes?"

"Si, it's Diana." It irritated him that she always felt compelled to identify herself when she called, as if he wouldn't recognize her voice after having been married to her for almost ten years.

"Yeah, hi," he said. He reached automatically for a smoke, then remembered and stopped. He had the fleeting thought that the wonderful St. Dr. Brogan could increase his fortunes if he'd come up with something that would kill the craving for nicotine. "What's up?"

He hoped nothing else needed fixing at the house. A month ago she'd ruined his only full day off in two weeks by asking him to work on the roof. There was a leak over the utility room.

When he'd pointed out that it wasn't *his* house any longer, and therefore should not continue to be his responsibility, Diana had pointed out in turn (rather icily) that his daughter still lived there, and that the dress she'd intended to wear to a party that afternoon had been sopping wet and stained, and that it was likely to happen again if he didn't fix the leak.

He'd wound up buying Patty a new dress (he'd never been able to bear seeing her cry, and now that he was with her so infrequently, it was even less bearable) and fixed the roof. He wished to God Diana would get herself another man. Not that it didn't give him a twinge or three, thinking about *his wife* with another man, in his house—being stepfather to his daughter—but she'd always needed a man, just not a *cop*. As long as they both lived in the same town, he supposed Diana would continue calling on him for assistance, saying she couldn't afford to hire someone. And it would always come down to hurting Patty in some way, if he didn't do it.

"I'm sorry, Si, I really am," Diana was saying, and it occurred to him that most of their conversations these days opened with those identical words. "I'd thought Mother would be able to take Patty today, only she's twisted her ankle and Dad's going to take her over to the emergency room for X rays to make sure it's only a sprain. I made this date weeks ago, and I was going to pick Patty up at Mother's Sunday morning. I hate to cancel the date, it's important to me. So I wondered, if it wouldn't be imposing too much—you are off today, aren't you? Could you keep Patty overnight?"

So there was another man, Si thought. And she was going somewhere with him overnight. He didn't know if that made his stomach turn over, or if it was just his hunger for a smoke that made him suddenly queasy.

"Si?"

"Yeah, I'm here. Sure, I'll take her. I don't suppose you could drop her by here?"

"Well, yes, if it's inconvenient for you to pick her up at home." There was a small silence, during which he said nothing, and she spoke more crisply. "We'll have her there in half an hour."

We, she'd said. He wondered who it was, hoped it was nobody he knew, then said to himself, "What the hell difference does it make? She's not married to me anymore."

He'd planned to do a little jogging today, he'd already put on sweat pants and shirt and his Nikes, and he wondered if Patty would like to go to the park so he could run a little, anyway. He couldn't go all the way around the track, because he wouldn't leave her alone while he did it. Still, he wasn't getting enough exercise these days, what with driving a cab for twelve hours when he wasn't sitting parked in it watching a motel.

He did a few push-ups and chin-ups while he was waiting. He'd better start working out more regularly, he decided.

He was standing at the window when the car drove up and Diana got out. The driver wasn't clearly visible, but it was definitely a man. The car was a year-old bronze Impala.

Patty got out of the back door, kissed Diana good-bye, and ran toward the door of the apartment house. Diana, without so much as a look upward toward his window to see if he were watching, got into the car, and it drove away. The angle was such that he couldn't get the license number.

Damn her, he thought angrily, striding toward the door to the top of the stairs, where he could hear his small daughter's light steps. How could any mother, let alone one who's been married to a cop, just send a little girl inside an apartment house without making sure she was getting to her destination safely?

"Hi, Daddy!" Patty called.

"Hi, Patty-cake. Come on up, I'm just cleaning up from breakfast. You can wash the dishes for me."

She came clomping up the stairs, dressed in a jogging outfit: bright red pants and sweatshirt and red and white Adidas. Her face was wreathed in a grin.

"How'd you like to go to the park, after we get the place in shape?" he demanded, swinging her off her feet when she reached the top.

"Okay." She looked around and giggled when he put her down inside the apartment. "Mama says you're a slob."

"Well, tell her thanks a lot. I don't have a maid, and I don't sit around on my butt all day watching soap operas, and I do the best I can," he said, and was immediately ashamed of having revealed his annoyance to the child. "Here, put an apron on"—he tied a dish towel around her middle—"and take care of the dishes. I'll change the bed and run the vacuum cleaner, and then we'll go, okay?"

"Can we have hot dogs for lunch?" Patty demanded, shoving up her sleeves before plunging her arms into the soapy water.

"I think this time we better have a well-balanced meal. I know, we'll go to the deli, and get stuff for a picnic."

It was at the delicatessen across from the park that he encountered the redhead, Erin Randall.

He had turned around to look at some specialty cheeses and he stepped on her foot. She emitted a small yelp, and Si spun, apology already flowing, when he recognized her.

"Hey, I'm sorry. I should have been looking. Did I hurt you?"

Her voice was rather low-pitched, infinitely appealing. "No, not really. These aren't steel-toed boots, though." She wiggled her foot experimentally. "No broken bones, I guess."

"I sure hope not. I'm really sorry." He liked her smile, and was sorry when she turned away to study the meats available for sandwiches. Making his own selections, he studied her unobtrusively.

"Mom, can I have baloney?"

He saw the little girl with her, then. A year or so older than

Patty, he guessed, and a genuine beauty with red-gold curls and a ready smile. She was pointing to her choice behind the glass.

Erin Randall laughed. "Baloney? When we're celebrating my new job? I'm going to have pastrami. You sure you want baloney?"

Silas stood watching her as she collected her order and left, heading for the park. At that moment he decided to pursue an acquaintance with her. She worked in that place, and even if she didn't know what the hell was going on there, she was in a position to find out. The feeling continued to grow, with little or no logic or evidence, that there *was* something wrong at Forest Hills, that Tillie's intuition, as well as his own, might be right.

It wasn't difficult at all. The Randalls were picnicking in the park too, and the kids were about the same age. Silas deliberately chose a table near the swings, several tables away from Erin Randall, and let the little girls get acquainted while they played.

He studied Erin's profile as she sat reading, oblivious of him, deciding that she was really a beautiful woman. A married woman. Well, hell, his interest in her wasn't romantic, was it? He was interested because she worked at Forest Hills.

"Daddy, I'm hungry!" Patty threw herself against his knees.

"It's only eleven o'clock. If we eat now, you'll be hungry again before suppertime."

"I'm hungry, too," the Randall girl said. She stood right behind Patty. "Why can't we eat together? There's plenty of room at our table. Where's your lunch, Patty? It's all right, isn't it, Mom, if we eat together?"

Erin lifted her head and looked at them, her eyes meeting Si's, smiling. Her hesitation was visible, yet brief. "Sure, why not?"

They spread their deli containers out on the table, and traded samples of cheeses and pickles, letting the kids do most of the talking at first. When there was an opportunity, Silas said casually, "I couldn't help overhearing, back at the deli, that you're celebrating a new job."

"Yes. I'd been working two part-time jobs ever since my husband died, which still only meant about half a salary, until I got this position at Forest Hills. It's a convalescent hospital."

Something twisted inside him, too strong to be ignored. She was a widow, not a married woman.

"I know the place. Out on Beverly Boulevard. You like it?"

"Love it," Erin said. "Have you tried these pickles? Kosher dills, they're marvelous."

He waited his opportunity to slip in his own marital status, now that he'd discovered hers. No doubt she took him for a married man; she'd be more friendly, maybe, if she didn't think he was married. Or, of course, it could work the other way around, but he didn't think so. He tended to go with his gut instincts.

"We don't get much time together anymore," Silas said, while the girls were feeding crackers to a squirrel. "Patty lives with her mother through the week, and half the time I'm working weekends. We used to do things like this a lot."

Erin's face was soft with emotion as she watched the girls. "We did too. When Ted was alive we had a lot of fun together, as a family. Nothing's been much fun since. I hope this job lasts, because the pay's so good, and it will mean we can do things again, simple things like picnics and movies." She looked at him then. "You're divorced. I suppose that's almost as bad as losing somebody to death, isn't it?"

"It hurts," Silas admitted. "Listen, does Sammie like the zoo? We went only a couple of weeks ago, but Patty loves it. Would you be interested in going with us? The kids seem to have hit it off pretty well."

"I haven't been to the zoo since Ted was killed."

"Killed?" he echoed, then wondered if he'd sounded too sharp. He almost asked if her husband had had any connection with Forest Hills.

"His car was hit broadside by a truck that lost its brakes," Erin said quietly. "He had no chance at all."

"Rough," Silas said. He wondered if he should mention the zoo again or let it drop. He didn't want to push, not yet.

Suddenly she smiled directly at him. "We'd love to go to the zoo with you," she said, and Silas felt something release inside of him.

He had a foot in the door. Now all he had to do was figure out how to get her to cooperate in finding out what in hell went on in that perfect rest home operated by the flawless Dr. Matthew Brogan.

It wasn't until he got home that he realized he hadn't even thought of smoking, all day.

12.

Erin was beginning to feel comfortable in the job. It wasn't particularly difficult, dealing with the patients' families. They were anxious, feeling guilty about committing their parents when those parents were upset about being put into a rest home, and she learned quickly how to deal with those feelings.

Unlike many rest homes where patients went unvisited for months, some of them for years, at Forest Hills this was not the case. If relatives didn't visit on a reasonable basis—say, a minimum of once a week—part of Erin's job was to give them a friendly call of reminder. (Dr. Brogan discussed this with the families ahead of time, in the same matter-of-fact way he put forth his policies regarding payment.) If there were no relatives, the calls went to friends. It was also up to Erin to coordinate visiting and entertainments by community and church groups, something she was doing rather by feel, since Sylvia hadn't had time to go into much detail about that aspect of the job. There were, of course, records of agencies that had helped out in the past, with phone numbers and names of those to contact.

The only patient who didn't seem genuinely pleased to be at Forest Hills was Ernie Denton. His daughter came several times a week, and probably would have come daily if he hadn't been so abusive whenever she walked through the doorway. He refused to join the others at meals, where he might have made friends, though as soon as the workmen had finished the room in the basement for his trains, he'd been well enough to go *there*. Janet took him down in the elevator, as a safety precaution—"Can you imagine getting him up, if he ever fell?" she'd asked, rolling her eyes—though he managed to walk fairly well once he got down there. The trains were assembled on a huge table so that he could get at everything without having to get down on the floor. They *were* fascinating, Erin thought; everybody on the staff except Dr.

Spaulding went down to look at them, even Dr. Brogan, and many of the patients did too.

"You'd have thought he'd have enjoyed showing them off to the others, and that *that* might have been an opening to make friends," Janet said. "But he's such a nasty old man—I'm glad not all my patients are like him."

Erin delivered mail to him nearly every day; if she couldn't be there in person, Paula Lundstrom was conscientious about sending him little notes and clever cards, though he never acknowledged any satisfaction from any of this. Erin felt sorry for Janet, who had to spend so much more time with him.

Still, the others were so nice they made up for Mr. Denton. She could see where she was likely to become quite attached to most of them.

The job was pleasant, the money made her almost limp with relief—though the first funds vanished like rain into parched earth for "essentials" they'd been doing without for so long—and her personal life began to seem at least minimally worthwhile again.

Not that anything special had really happened, she told herself. She'd met that nice Mr. Copetti in the park, and they'd taken the girls to the zoo and had a lovely, normal afternoon.

That was it, normal, she thought. She'd been alone since Ted's death, more alone than she'd realized. Having Sammie to talk to didn't alleviate the need for adult conversation and companionship, and though Ruth was warm and considerate, she wasn't the answer.

Well, face it, Erin thought. For nine years she'd had a husband, a lover, a friend. They'd done things as a family, had laughed a lot, and she'd known he loved her. They'd always been perfectly compatible in bed, and she'd missed that terribly; not just the lovemaking, but the closeness, the sharing of thoughts and ideas as well as the cuddling.

She knew Sammie missed the displays of affection too; she and Ted had been very close. "My daughter-son," he'd called her, teasingly. "My little girl, with the boy's name," for he'd called her Sam. Erin had tried to increase her own demonstrativeness since Ted's death; it was important to a child to feel loved and wanted, to be caressed and hugged often. Yet she'd seen Sammie's response to Si Copetti, that eagerness to get his attention. She needed a father.

Not that Erin looked upon Copetti as a possible suitor. How could she, after such a casual meeting? He hadn't even suggested they get together again. But she'd enjoyed the day, and that indicated to her that maybe she was ready to try to rebuild something in the way of a social life. See a man, or several men. Go out once in a while and remember she was a woman, not just a mother.

Of course dating would be complicated by the fact that she had a child. Reliable sitters were hard to come by, and she knew, even before the necessity arose, that she'd hesitate to ask Ruth to keep Sammie if she went out with another man. Ruth wouldn't say anything about it, she was sure, but the idea made her uncomfortable; it was as if dating would signify that she'd forgotten Ted.

And how did she meet an eligible man in the first place? She'd encountered dozens of men when she worked evenings at the bowling alley, and a lot of them had flirted with her, even made obvious passes. Yet most of them had worn wedding rings, and none had made her seriously consider seeing them away from the alleys.

She'd hoped there might be an employee at the hospital, but there wasn't. Oh, Dr. Brogan was currently unattached, and from what Sylvia had said she thought he was not immune to a pretty face, but he was too old for her, even if it hadn't been well known that he thought two marriages were enough. Dr. Spaulding, whom she'd seen only once, was too old also, and singularly unattractive. In fact, he'd made so little impression that she was sure if she met him on the street, without his lab coat, she'd never recognize him.

Today the mail was late, and then she got delayed because a patient was checking out. Mrs. Tosta, smiling, saying good-byes all around to the staff, left on the arm of her son.

"I can't believe how much better you look," he told her.

"And how much better I feel. Don't look for me back for a long time," she told the nurses and aides.

When the Tostas had driven away, Erin belatedly made the rounds with the mail. She paused first in the open doorway at Dr. Brogan's office and found him absorbed in the morning paper, a half-frown on his face.

Erin stepped forward and saw that he was looking at the obituary page. Quietly, she placed the mail on his desk; only then did he seem aware of her.

"Oh, Erin. Thank you."

"Is there something wrong?" she asked, then wondered if she should have voiced her concern.

He removed his glasses and rubbed at the marks they'd left on his nose. "Not wrong, exactly. She was ill, had a stroke, and it's not surprising that she died, but it's always a shock when someone dies. You never get used to it, no matter how often you see it."

"I'm sorry," Erin said. "A former patient?"

"Well, I did treat her initially when she had the stroke, though she was transferred to San Cristobal General almost immediately. She was our bookkeeper, a very nice and very efficient lady." He pushed the paper aside. "I guess I'd better get down to business."

She left him opening a chart from the stack that appeared there every morning in exchange for the ones Lois had carried away. The bookkeeper, he'd said. What had Sylvia called her? Mrs. Masterson, wasn't that it?

How sad, that both she and Sylvia had died. She supposed she was going to be around when some of the patients died, and she didn't look forward to it a bit. The smart thing would be not to allow herself to get too involved, but how did you manage that when you were a warmhearted person? It was easy to imagine herself as old and sick, separated from family and friends, needing kindness and compassion from strangers.

It was so late that lunch trays were being passed around to the few patients who didn't eat in the dining room. Janet had just delivered one to Ernie Denton when Erin entered with his mail.

"Well," she said brightly, "are you having a birthday or something? You have seven letters today."

He scowled at her. "Wasting their time. My will's already made out. Left everything to Paula, though damned if I know why. Just because she's my only child. If my son had lived, he wouldn't have put me in this goddamned place." He waved a hand at her letters. "Nephews, nieces, people I haven't heard from in years—getting in their last licks when they think I'm dying. Not a one of them gives a good goddamn if I do, long as I mention them in my will first. Hell of a lot of good it does to have the money; it won't get me out of this place."

Erin put the envelopes on the table beside his tray, and for the first time really paid attention to what a patient ate.

She knew that reducing his weight was a major part of his treatment—in fact, it was possible to see that he had lost weight in the short time he'd been here, because his face was less fleshy, though the mound of abdomen did not seem diminished—yet this hardly seemed like a diet plate. "My, that looks appetizing," she commented, smiling.

"Fish," he snarled. "Second time this week."

"Fish and poultry are high on the lists," Erin admitted. "They're considered to be better for us than red meats. And you have parslied potatoes, cole slaw, buttered carrots, and some sort of soup. And pie for dessert?"

He made no move to pick up spoon or fork. "You know where my clothes are?"

"No, I'm afraid I don't. You aren't considering leaving us, are you, Mr. Denton?" She kept her tone light, covering her sense of revulsion at the loose, thick-lipped mouth, the puffy fingers.

"Give me my goddamned pants and I'll get out of here soon enough. Tell that nurse I want the bedpan."

He was perfectly able to walk to the bathroom unaided, she knew that. Yet she wasn't in control of his medical problems, only assigned to deliver the mail, and she was content to leave it at that rather than make a stand against him.

"Yes, of course," she said softly, and left him there with the lunch that made her hungry to look at it.

She paused at the nurses' station, and Joan Warlum nodded. "He does this every mealtime. Then he complains that the food is cold, and insists that he have another tray from the kitchen."

Erin hesitated, curious. "Does he get it?"

"Usually. He wouldn't if it were up to me," Joan said crisply. "You delivering anything today to Mrs. Hampton? She's feeling poorly, could use a lift."

Erin sifted through the stack. "Yes, two."

"Good. See if you can talk her into a better humor before I have to administer her injection. She always fusses. The only one worse than she is, is Mr. Denton. I've been nursing for years, and he's the only patient I've ever had that I had to force myself to touch."

"A hard man to like," Erin agreed as she moved away.

She hadn't taken mail to Mrs. Hampton for perhaps a week—though she had relatives who came frequently, she got little mail—and Erin was surprised at the woman's appearance.

Mrs. Hampton looked wan and, astonishingly, thinner. Erin had no idea what was the matter with her, aside from extreme obesity, but she seemed far less robust than previously.

She was listless, not very interested in her mail, nor in conversation. Erin walked on down the corridor, until all the letters had been delivered, then went to lunch. Mrs. Hampton's tray had been there too, though virtually untouched. She wondered how they could lose weight on such meals, complete with desserts. If she ever needed to go on a diet, she'd ask what their secret was here, she thought in amusement.

13.

Ernie Denton had never felt more miserable, and more desperate, in his life.

In his daughter's house he'd done as he pleased. He'd eaten what he wanted, when he wanted it; if the kitchen couldn't supply his needs, he'd had a phone at his elbow to order it brought in from outside. He had gone to sleep when he liked, sat all day in front of the TV if that was his pleasure, and had not been hassled by determinedly cheerful young women who stuck pills in his mouth and needles in his behind.

God, those hypocritical smiling faces. They smiled at you no matter what they were going to do to you, and kept on smiling afterward while you groaned or bellowed in pain, and said stupid things like "There, that wasn't so bad, was it?"

What good was a beautifully appointed room when you had no privacy, nothing to say about what was done to you or for you? When you were so goddamned hungry all the time that you thought you'd rather die than go on this way?

He'd looked for his clothes and didn't find them. When he demanded to know where they were, Janet informed him that his daughter had taken them home since he didn't want to dress and go downstairs.

He decided he would go downstairs, then, at least to the basement. Paula brought back his pants and shirts, socks and underwear, and some sweaters. He was cold all the time, he needed the sweaters.

The first time he got dressed, disdaining assistance from Janet, he was amazed to see that his belt had to be tightened two full notches. He'd known they were starving him, but he hadn't thought he'd lost an inch and a half from around his middle. His shirt flapped loosely too.

He saw nothing grossly unattractive about his own body.

Couldn't expect a man to stay slim forever, and what difference did it make when he was eighty-two and probably dying pretty soon anyway? He took no satisfaction in the evidence of weight loss; it only proved what he already knew, that they were starving him.

The first time he went down to the dining room, everybody looked at him. He discovered two things: first, when he ignored them, they didn't pay any attention to him either, which was fine. The second thing was more important. Food was served family style, in bowls on the table where each diner could help himself. Obviously, if he ate here, he could eat more than they'd been bringing him on the trays.

The first time he took six eggs and four pieces of toast and four sausages, he watched warily to see if anyone would stop him. Nobody appeared to be paying any attention except a birdlike little woman directly across the table, whose eyes widened a trifle. Ernie Denton glared at her, and she looked down at her own plate.

When a bowl or a platter was emptied, a pretty little brunette came and lifted the container, asking, "Did everyone have enough?"

The first three meals he didn't have nerve enough to ask for more. Though the little bird-woman hadn't looked directly at him through the remainder of his meals, he knew she'd kept track of what he ate. Would she speak up, if he said he was still hungry, and announce how much he'd already had?

And then, after working up to it all night when he couldn't sleep because he kept thinking about food, he told the girl, "Yes, I'd like more pancakes."

"All right, sir," she said, smiling, and damned if she didn't bring in another whole platter of them, buckwheats, with a choice of honey, maple syrup, or blueberry jam to put on them. For the first time since he'd come here, he ended a meal feeling satisfied.

Unfortunately, the sense of fullness didn't last long. He learned to be the last to leave the table, and when the others were shuffling out, paying no attention to him, he took his napkin and wrapped up whatever was left and stuck it inside his shirt. More often than not, at breakfast, it was only a few slices of toast, or a couple of sweet rolls, or some fruit or melon. At lunch and dinner, the pickings were somewhat better. There were more rolls, and a few chops or slices of meat loaf or a chicken breast to be hoarded against starvation.

He hid the food in the drawer of his nightstand, and then had to remember not to ask the aide for anything from that drawer.

He became obsessed with the idea of escaping this hospital/prison. He demanded pencil and paper, and began to make intricate notes about schedules: where each of the nurses and aides were at particular times, when everyone gathered in the dining room, when each of the patients went to bed, the movements of the staff after lights-out at ten or thereabouts.

He suffered, though not in silence, the indignity of being taken up and down between floors in a wheelchair. He was allowed to get out of it and sit in a regular chair in the dining room, as well as to walk wherever he liked in the basement.

This area had been turned into a cedar-paneled, carpeted recreation room, with the gigantic table in the middle for his trains. There were several couches and chairs, and a stereo. And that silly bitch of a daughter of his had paid for the entire thing with his money, he thought. Nobody had asked him if he wanted it done. Nobody ever asked him what he thought about anything.

It was *his* room, though, in the basement; no one came there after the first day or so, because he made it a point to ensure that they knew they were not welcome.

Unfortunately, there was no way to the outside from the basement. He found a furnace room and storage areas off the rec room, but the windows were all far too small to permit the passage of anyone of his bulk, even if he'd had the strength to try such an escape.

What he needed was an ordinary door, one that wasn't locked.

He was unable to find one.

Once during afternoon visiting hours, when there were a fair number of people wandering through the corridors, he tried to walk out the front door. The redheaded receptionist called his name and came after him. For a moment he thought she'd grab his arm, and he'd made up his mind that if she did, he'd knock her flat, but at the last moment she drew back and moved quickly past him to the doorway. A few seconds after that, the security man *did* cut him off, and Ernie knew he was no match for *him*.

It was later that evening, when his cache of goodies produced nothing better than a stale bun, that it occurred to him that by this time of day the kitchen ought to be empty. They thought he was senile, and they treated him the way they'd treat a valuable but disliked show dog: they protected him, even from himself, and assumed that he was brainless.

It wouldn't do to allow them to think otherwise.

He consulted his notes, then placed them back in their hiding place in the bedpan. (He had given up asking for the bedpan. He wanted to convince them he could walk so they'd stop insisting on the goddamned wheelchair, though he was canny enough to realize that it wouldn't do to appear *too* mobile.)

The nurse, that snotty one with the thick glasses whose name he couldn't be bothered to recall, was at her station, talking to the aide. Ernie stood in the doorway of his darkened room, hearing a few voices besides those of the women he could see. He had to pass the nurse to get to the elevator.

He didn't have to wait long. A light went on at his end of the corridor, and he stepped backward into the shadows. The lights had been dimmed out there, too, and the aide didn't look at him as she went past, moving swiftly on rubber-soled shoes. It was Mrs. Hampton's room, and nobody ever got away from that old crow in less than ten minutes, he thought. It was one of the things he'd taken note of.

The head nurse was still there, and after a few seconds another light went on, at the opposite end of the hallway. The old witch stood up and headed for it.

As soon as she disappeared into Mr. Melbourne's room, Ernie Denton bolted for the elevator. The door slid smoothly shut behind him; even if anyone noticed now that it was descending, there would be no reason to question who was in it.

He hoped his wheezing wouldn't be audible to anyone on the main floor when the doors eased silently open.

Except for the night-lights, the place was dark and deserted. He made his shambling way toward the rear of the building, seeing the dim glow of small bulbs in various offices, passing the darkened dining rooms—one for patients, one for staff—and then pushed open the door into the kitchen.

There were enough lights on here. He made a beeline for the outside door, only to find that it was locked. He'd hoped maybe there'd be a lock that could be disengaged from the inside without a key. Well, to hell with them, then. Sooner or later there'd be a way out, especially if they didn't suspect him. At least he'd get something to eat now.

The refrigerator yielded assorted cold cuts, cheeses, a pair of chops, and even a bottle of wine. He looked at the wine with regret; he'd never get away with that, since he'd have to dispose of the bottle, and it couldn't be flushed away. He settled for several snorts and put it back.

The pantry made his rheumy old eyes light up. My God, they had everything in here, and in such quantity that no one could keep up with it. Nobody'd miss a few cartons of crackers and cookies, the tins of sardines and corned beef, the Hershey bars and marinated artichoke hearts and olives. He filled his shirt, then decided he could carry more, and more safely, on a regular tray. He'd hide it tonight, then set it out in the morning and pretend one of the aides had left it there during the night shift.

He remembered to appropriate a can opener, and a fork for the artichoke hearts. He didn't mind using his fingers on most things, but artichoke hearts were messy; someone would be bound to wonder about oily drippings on his pajama front.

It wasn't until he'd safely gained the elevator that it occurred to him that when the elevator doors opened, directly opposite the nurses' desk, he might well be caught.

He hesitated, not pushing the button to send the cubicle upward. He couldn't manage the stairs, he hadn't climbed even a few steps for years without wheezing; several times Paula had called an aid car, with oxygen, he got so bad.

He wished he'd brought his notes with him; he tried to remember them. At 10:30, when everyone was usually settled down, didn't the staff usually retire to their little kitchen for a coffee break? What time was it now?

It was difficult to see his watch without spilling stuff off the tray, but he managed it: 10:35.

He nudged the elevator button with his elbow, and began to move upward. Except for his own raspy breathing, there was no sound at all. When the doors slid open, the chairs behind the desk were empty.

With the speed and grace of a giant crab, Ernie Denton sidled down the hallway to his room.

14.

Two weeks passed before Silas made contact with Erin Randall again. He thought about her a lot and considered various methods of approach—probably just calling her up and asking her out was as good as anything—but he didn't have time to follow through.

He met George Walker when he picked him up in the cab one day and took him to work. Walker's car was in the shop for some bodywork and Mrs. Walker needed the other car. He turned out to own the largest department store in San Cristobal, and he'd just seen inventory figures which convinced him that shoplifting in the store was getting totally out of hand.

When, during a traffic tie-up because of an accident, he learned that Copetti was a private investigator and an ex-cop, Mr. Walker was impressed by the advice that Silas offered and made a counter-suggestion.

"Why don't you come into my store, and see what you can do for me? I'm not a poor man, but I sure as hell will be if they keep ripping me off this way. I need professional help."

Three days later Silas entered George Walker's office with information and recommendations. "You're getting some shoplifting, all right, though not an excessive amount, considering the size of your operation. Most of your loss is through these three employees. They're robbing you blind."

He laid the list of names on Walker's desk, watched the man go first pale and then livid. "You're certain? Even Jeffers? My manager?"

Silas put down another list. "Here's what he's taken out of here in three days. Multiply that by ten and you've got what he's costing you per month. How long's he worked for you?"

"Twelve years," Walker said, sounding strangled. "Christ, I can't believe it. Can we prove it? Can I prosecute him?"

"I can prove this much. We can set him up and prove something more, and sure, you can prosecute him. You probably won't get your money back, but you'll slow down the thefts. The other two, the women, are obviously thieves of long-standing, too. Just getting rid of the three of them will stop a big drain. Then I'd suggest some training of the remaining employees to know how to handle the petty theft and the professional shoplifting. You could use a full-time security guard or two; the savings would more than pay their salaries."

He spent the remainder of that week getting the goods on the store manager, two more days to wrap up the two women, and a three-hour, after-closing session with the staff on prevention of theft. His fee was substantial. Not only that, but within the next few days he had three more calls from other store owners or managers for similar services. He hardly drove the cab at all except in the evenings.

He dropped in at Smitty's on Saturday night and found Grady in his customary booth. Grady waved him in. "Waiting for Cheryl to get off shift. How's it going, Si?"

"Not too bad. What's happening with you?"

Grady grinned. "I'm making progress. Hey, you get the message I left on your machine?"

"Yeah. I never found time to call you back, but thanks. Anything new on that front?"

Grady's grin faded and he lowered his voice, hunching over his drink. "Oh, the shit's in the fan and it's splattering far and wide. Mitchum's got his feet in the trough again, only this time I don't think he's going to get away with it. He tried to deal with the wrong party, tread on the wrong toes, and he was called before the grand jury yesterday and committed perjury before he realized Chief Malone himself was an opposing witness. They haven't handed down a verdict yet, but the betting's heavy that this time the son of a bitch is going down for the count."

Silas sipped at the head on his beer. "Too bad I didn't have Malone testifying against him when I had *my* tail in the crack."

"Yeah. I think it's pretty sure, Si. Mitchum is on his way out." Grady hesitated, then said tentatively, "The department is already short one man, and if Mitchum goes—and Claudius will probably take the fall with him—we'll be down another two men."

Silas stared at him. "What's that got to do with me? I'm *persona non grata* with the San Cristobal P.D. There's no way in hell I'll ever get back on the force."

Grady wiped his mouth with the back of one hand, quiet and curiously intense. "There might be, Si. You know Malone always liked you. He didn't want to let you go, I know that because I heard him say so, but hell, the evidence against you was strong. Mitchum lied in his teeth so you'd take the fall, and Malone couldn't believe both of you. When it's a captain against a sergeant, you know who's going to get stuck."

"He isn't going to do a turnaround now, just because Mitchum finally screwed up."

"He might, Si. Would you be interested in rejoining S.C.P.D. if it turned out to be possible?"

For a moment he couldn't reply, only staring into Grady's face. When he did speak, his words were husky. "Hell, yes. Only I don't intend to get my guts all churned up again for nothing, buddy. I was eviscerated the last time around, and I'm getting too old to go through that again."

"Well, nothing will happen until the grand jury decides whether or not to indict Mitchum. Katolik's dating Malone's youngest daughter, did you know that? Megan, the cute one?"

"I thought she was about thirteen years old."

"No, no, she's eighteen now. And they're serious, talking marriage. Katolik's in a position to talk to Chiefie informally, off the record, see what he says. Only he told me he didn't want to do it unless you really wanted back on the force. No sense sticking his neck out unless there's a point to it."

For a moment Silas was silent, aware of a churning in his gut.

"You say the word, and we'll sound out the old man. There's no hard evidence against you in the files, Si. They didn't indict you for anything."

"They might as well have," Si said, unable to put down his bitterness, though he knew that an indictment, a conviction on false charges, would have been far worse than being asked to resign.

"Whatta you say, buddy?" Grady asked softly, and Silas sighed.

"Hell, yes, I'd give a year of my life to get back on the force."

Grady's face split in a grin. "I'll get back to you, first news I have. Next week, probably."

Silas left the bar feeling very peculiar, as if a toe that had been numb for years had suddenly come to life with a painful tingling. Only it wasn't just a toe, it was his whole body.

It was supposed to be his weekend to have Patty, but Diana called to say she had a bad cold and shouldn't be out in this rainy weather; would it be all right if he took her the next two weekends, providing she got over her cold and didn't get bronchitis as she sometimes did?

Silas agreed—what else could he do?—and wondered, if he kept getting work with local businesses, if he could afford a better place to live. Well, hell, he knew he could afford something better than the present rattrap; he'd moved into the first place he'd seen and never cared enough to get out and find something better. But it wasn't a place he wanted to bring Patty, not for the weekend, if there was no planned excursion of some kind.

He missed having the kid around while he did chores or read the papers. This taking her on weekends, running to the park or the zoo or a kids' movie, that wasn't a natural relationship to have with your daughter. He needed a decent place to live where they could have an ordinary life. He even went so far as to check the classified ads.

It was hard to believe what they got for two-bedroom apartments. A house was out of the question for now, though that was what he'd have liked best: a place with a backyard for swings and a safe place to play. He thought about the house that he and Diana had bought, the house they'd dreamed of for years, and supposed he ought to be glad he wasn't still having to make the payments on it. Diana had a good job, so all he was stuck with was child support, and he didn't begrudge that. He did begrudge the loss of the house, though. It had been *his* dream house too.

When the phone rang as he was about to leave for a run in the park, he almost didn't answer it. If it was Diana again, he didn't really want to talk to her.

It was Aunt Tillie. "Silas, dear, we're all getting together at my place tomorrow for lasagna. Why don't you join us? We haven't seen you in weeks."

"Oh, I don't know, I have some things I need to do . . ." He'd always enjoyed the family gatherings, but now it hurt to see the other guys with their wives and kids, and the aunts and cousins were beginning to try to fix him up with somebody. "I think I'll pass this time, though I'll miss your famous lasagna."

She wanted to talk, so he leaned against the wall and listened, resisting the urge to light a cigarette. She told him who was pregnant, and who was getting married—his cousin Sally was both— and who had changed jobs. And then Tillie said, "Did you ever find out any more about that hospital where Isadore was?"

"I don't think there's anything to find out," Silas told her. "Dr. Brogan and the whole place check out squeaky clean."

Tillie made a murmuring sound. "I suppose it's only because I was so sure he was going to get well. You're right, people die in a place like that all the time. It's hard to realize you're in an age group where everybody's dying. Of course Mrs. Lombard was older than I am—the paper said eighty-four—but she didn't seem older. She was such a nice lady. I used to stop and talk to her sometimes; her room was right next to Isadore's."

Silas caught his hand reaching for the pack of cigarettes beside the phone and stopped. "What's this about a Mrs. Lombard? She was a patient at Forest Hills and she died?"

"Yes. It was in today's paper. And Mrs. Masterson, too, only she wasn't old. Only fifty-six. You don't expect somebody fifty-six to die."

He heard his voice sharpen involuntarily. "This Mrs. Masterson was a patient there, too?"

"No, no, she worked in the office. Bookkeeping, I think. She explained the bills to me. She died a couple of weeks ago. I read where the family didn't want flowers, but asked that donations be made to Forest Hills. She must have known she was dying—ahead of time, I mean."

When he hung up, Silas reached for the pack again, and this time allowed himself to follow through and take a cigarette and light it. Another patient wasn't surprising—given the ages of the patients at Forest Hills it would be surprising if they *didn't* die off —but what was this about a Mrs. Masterson, age fifty-six?

A couple of weeks ago, Tillie had said. He turned toward the pile of newspapers that had been accumulating and searched until he found it. Of course the obituary didn't tell him any more than

Tillie had. It didn't really mean anything, that two employees of the place had died recently.

But it started to bug him again. He smoked the butt down to the filter, then let himself out of the apartment. He wondered if Erin Randall would have noticed yet if there was something fishy going on at Forest Hills, and decided to give her a call when he got home.

15.

Erin had, ever so slightly, hoped that Silas Copetti would call her after the day they'd spent together at the park and the zoo, entertaining the kids. When he didn't, she was philosophical about it, though she'd liked him and hoped that it was mutual.

He slid into the back of her mind, however; there were plenty of other things to think about. For one thing, a larger apartment became available in her building, one with two bedrooms so that she didn't have to share with Sammie anymore. She got two of Ted's brothers to come and haul the heavy stuff downstairs for her; they set up her king-sized bed, and Al made a crack about not needing it unless she was going to have company. This was said with a leer that made it clear she could have *his* company if she chose.

Erin had learned to ignore Al's offensive behavior, and wondered how his wife had stood it all these years; he never seemed to care whether she overheard him or not, and she always took it in stride, though she must have been humiliated beyond measure.

She brushed this remark aside as she had always done. Ted had been convinced that his brother meant no offense, that it was simply his way of joking, and he was harmless. Erin hadn't bothered to tell her husband how his brother had gotten her squashed up against the washing machine when he had an obvious hard-on, making suggestions that hadn't sounded harmless at all. He hadn't really frightened her, because his wife and his mother were both in the kitchen only a few yards away and she'd assumed that if she'd screamed she wouldn't have been raped with those two as an audience.

She'd never cared for Al, but she wasn't afraid of him as long as the third brother, Bobby, was around too. And there was no one else she could think of, without hiring it done, to get her moved.

The apartment was not only larger, it was nicer. There was room for her dining-room set, as well as the rest of her living-room furniture, and the place had an entirely different atmosphere, she thought. Perhaps it was her own changed attitude, but she felt, well, *content*, for the first time since Ted's death.

It was strange, though, getting into the king-sized bed. Al was right about one thing, it wasn't intended for a lone sleeper. It felt entirely different from the twin to Sammie's bed. It felt lonely.

Now she knew she wanted another man. Not just any man, of course, but she wanted to be part of a couple again. Once she really felt secure in the job, she'd have to see what might be possible in the way of meeting people again.

There were several attractive men in her computer class who were friendly, but she wasn't sure they were even single. One thing she was sure of: what she was looking for was something permanent, a mutual commitment, not a mere fling.

Though no relationships developed at Forest Hills that led to socializing, she became better acquainted with the staff and liked them all. Even the nursing supervisor, Vonda Busby, who had at first intimidated her a little, was nice to her.

Vonda was very attractive, and very businesslike. She took her responsibilities seriously. According to the R.N.s and aides who worked under her, she was strict and had a hell of a temper, in an icy way, if you forgot somebody's catheter or allowed them to develop a bed sore. There were rumors that she was seeing Dr. Brogan after hours, but there was nothing in the behavior of either of them while at the hospital to suggest such a thing.

Vonda was drinking coffee in the staff dining room one morning when Erin took her own break, only the two of them there. For a moment Erin had hesitated, until the other woman looked up and smiled.

"Sit down. The coffee's fresh, and there are homemade cinnamon rolls, too."

"Umm. Wonderful. I'll have to start watching my waistline, if I indulge very often." Erin took a seat across the table from her.

Vonda laughed. "Yes. It's a hazard around here, when we have such a good cook. She's spoiled me for restaurant meals."

They sat talking, first of the patients, and then of more personal things. "I understand you have a little girl," Vonda said.

"Yes. Samantha. She's eight." On impulse, Erin reached for her purse and pulled out a picture. "That's her second-grade picture."

She was immediately embarrassed by this action. No stranger really wanted to look at pictures of unknown kids. But Vonda took it and studied it with seemingly genuine interest.

"She's lovely. You're lucky. I wanted a girl, but I got a boy."

"Oh, I didn't know you had a child too."

"Loren's sixteen. I had him when I was seventeen. I didn't even know I was pregnant until after his father had walked out on me and the marriage had been annulled. I'd taken my own name back again, and I hated him so much I wouldn't even give Loren his name. He thinks his father's dead, as he may be, by now. I haven't heard from him since he walked out the door half my lifetime ago."

Erin accepted her picture back. "Does he live with you? Your son?"

"No. I had to go to work, and my mother took him. When I decided to go to nursing school, she kept him on, and by the time I could afford to keep him, it was really too late for all of us. Mother didn't want to give him up, he knew her a lot better than he did me, and I'd still have had the problem of caring for him while I worked. So we decided it was better he stay with her in San Diego."

Erin imagined giving up Sammie and felt a flash of actual pain. "It must have been very hard to do."

"Yes." Vonda smiled. "He's cute, he really is. And very bright." Then she laughed. "I suppose all parents think that, don't they? Cute and bright. I talk to him on the phone about once a week, and he writes me letters. He used to send me pictures that he drew. He's been more like—a little brother, I guess. Lucky my mother was young enough to cope with him. He and my dad are great pals. A boy needs a man, so it's probably best for him where he is."

Several of the aides came in, and one of them, Karen, sat down next to Vonda. She reached over and pounced on the nursing supervisor's wrist.

"Oh, what a beautiful watch! Are those real diamonds?"

"Of course, silly," the other aide said, leaning forward to look more closely. "Wow! It's gorgeous, Miss Busby!"

"A gift?" Karen asked enviously, and Vonda laughed.

"I think it's more of a bribe. Or maybe the most accurate answer would be that it's a step in a seduction." She pushed back her chair and stood up. "Or what he hopes will be a seduction," she corrected.

They were all laughing when Erin, too, rose and left the table.

She felt at ease in the job. She hadn't made any stupid mistakes in the past week, she'd brought in what the patients said was some of the best entertainment they'd had, and Dr. Brogan had complimented her on her rapport with the patients.

On Friday night she and Sammie went out for pizza, and they took some to Ruth on the way home. It was a nice evening, relaxing and fun. It made her even more lonely when they got home and Sammie went to bed. It was only nine o'clock, and there was nothing to do except watch TV, which she wasn't in the mood for.

The phone rang as she started to unbutton her blouse.

Moderately alarmed—normally she had few telephone calls and none at this time of evening—Erin snatched it up. "Yes?"

"Mrs. Randall? Erin?"

She recognized his voice at once, and the tension eased out of her. "Yes. Silas Copetti, isn't it?"

"Well, good. You haven't forgotten me. I hope I'm not calling too late."

"No, no." She rebuttoned the blouse without thinking.

"I was wondering—I have Patty again tomorrow, and she and your Sammie got along so well together—would you like to go for a drive? Take a lunch and head up along the coast, maybe picnic on the beach somewhere? Make a day of it?"

Her voice revealed none of the exultation that swept through her. "Why, that sounds like fun. Yes, we'd like that."

"Good. Say about ten in the morning, then?"

"At ten. And since you're driving, I'll make the lunch. Do you like corned beef? And macaroni salad? I do a good one, with shrimp in it."

"Sounds great," Silas told her. "I'll see you tomorrow."

She supposed she ought to feel a little guilty about the fantasies she had after she'd gone to bed. But what the hell, that's what fantasies were for, wasn't it? To help you cope with not being able, or seriously wanting, to do something that circumstances or morals prevented you from doing. She only hoped that she wouldn't blush when she met Silas in the morning.

The day was as wonderful as she'd hoped it would be.

In late September, the weather was perfect: sunny, with a nip early in the day that continued to hang in the wind until midafternoon. It didn't bother them.

The Pacific was at its best, blue and thunderously frothy on the beach. They had it virtually to themselves, sharing only with the gulls and a pair of seals that bobbed offshore, looking like the spectators at some entertainment by the humans on shore.

They all ran on the firm sand at the waterline until they were winded. Then Silas and Erin found a sheltered spot behind a stack of heavy driftwood, where they sat and talked while watching the girls build castles in the wet sand a short distance away.

She didn't remember much of what they talked about; she only knew that it was pleasant and exciting to be in the presence of an attractive man whose gaze was clearly admiring.

Once he asked her lazily, "Still liking that job?" and she said, "Oh, yes, it's a great place to work." And then, when she was packing away the remains of their picnic and the girls had run shrieking toward a green glass float that came in on the tide, he rolled over and sat up and looked at her in a way that made her forget the lids on the Tupperware.

"You know, I think it would be fun to do something together, just you and me, without the kids. What do you like? Dancing? Eating out? Bowling? Movies? None of the above?"

She laughed. "*Any* of the above sounds good. I haven't done anything on an adult level in ages."

He leaned forward to examine her face at close proximity. "Your eyes really are green, aren't they? Listen, how adult you want to get?"

She felt her cheeks warm as she remembered last night's fantasies. "Well, not *too* adult."

"Can you get a sitter for tomorrow night?"

"Yes. I'm sure my mother-in-law will keep Sammie." She'd worry later about what Ruth would think.

"Okay. Let's make it dinner and a movie. A proper first date. I know people don't date anymore, but I have a hunch you're an old-fashioned girl, so let's do it. And afterward I'll take you home and we can have a drink before the fire—"

"No fireplace," Erin interrupted, laughing.

"—with the stereo playing something romantic, and we'll talk until two A.M."

"I have to get up and go to work on Monday morning," she reminded him, caught up in the spirit of the thing.

"Well, we could go to bed at eleven, but I don't think you're *that* kind of girl, either." His gaze was speculative. "Though I'd be happy to be proved wrong. Anyway, let's play that part by ear, okay?"

She wouldn't go to bed with him, Erin thought after he'd left her off at home that evening. She really *was* old-fashioned in that regard. She'd never slept with anybody but Ted in her life, and even if she hadn't believed that if you wanted marriage instead of one-night stands you'd better hold out for it, she thought a woman with kids ought to set a good example for them. How could you expect a child to see you with a live-in lover, or even a sleep-over one, and not think it was all right to have sex with anybody when her own turn came?

Only last week Sammie had come home and calmly announced that Mrs. Leighton, the mother of her best friend Kitty, had a live-in boyfriend. "Kitty says they go in the bedroom and lock the door sometimes. And they make so much noise at night that they keep her awake. What are they doing in there, Mom?"

She'd always thought that when Sammie started asking questions she'd answer them as fully and as truthfully as she could. Yet now the time was here, and she wasn't at all prepared. She'd said, "Oh, grown-up things. Maybe they're going to get married."

Sammie's red-gold curls bounced when she shook her head. "No. Mrs. Leighton says she's never going to get married again, because then that bastard would be able to stop paying alimony. That's what she always calls Kitty's dad, 'that bastard.' What's a bastard?"

"It's a name she's using for someone she doesn't like anymore. Not a very nice name," Erin added quickly, "so don't use it, okay?"

"I think he's very nice. Whenever I'm with Kitty and he comes over, or gives her a ride home from school, he buys me an ice-cream cone too. And he's funny. Only Mrs. Leighton can't stand him." The child sighed deeply. "Hardly anybody I know has both a mother and a father. Most of the fathers didn't die, like Daddy. They got divorced."

Erin hugged her. "You miss Daddy a lot, don't you? So do I."

The moment had passed, yet thinking about it now, Erin saw the pitfalls looming ahead of her. She supposed she'd more or less gone numb when Ted was killed. And now she was coming alive again. She was only thirty-two; she had a lot of years ahead of her, and she didn't want to spend them alone.

She wasn't going to go to bed with Silas Copetti, but she *was* strongly attracted to him, and there was a certain dangerous excitement in knowing that he'd be making a pass at her.

It turned out to be more dangerous than she'd expected.

Dinner was innocuous enough, with good food and conversation. She was surprised to find that he drove a cab, less surprised to learn that he'd been a police officer and now did private investigating. He seemed the kind of man who would be tough and capable.

"Why did you stop being a cop, if you liked it so much?" she asked, and was faced with a wry grin.

"I was asked to resign." He waited for her reaction to that, and when it was minimal, concern rather than shock, he added, "There was an interdepartmental mess, and I got left holding the bag. The only thing I was guilty of was bad judgment in trusting a superior officer, but I took the fall. Law enforcement was the only thing I was trained for, and somebody asked me to do a little investigating for him, and I just sort of fell into getting my license as a P.I."

"But you don't like it nearly as well as being a cop," Erin said, and saw that he was pleased at how perceptive she was.

"Yeah, I miss it. But that's the way life is, isn't it? Nobody gives you anything for keeps. You know that as well as I do."

The conversation drifted off in another direction; she felt relaxed and comfortable with him. She decided she liked Silas a lot.

The movie was one of the new science fiction ones with five million dollars worth of special effects. If they'd spent a fraction of that amount on getting a good writer to develop a plot, it could have been a sensational movie. As it was, they both enjoyed it anyway; Erin was beginning to think she'd enjoy just about anything in his company.

She didn't get nervous until she'd poured drinks in her own living room and went to sit down in the big easy chair at right angles to the couch where Silas sat.

"Uh-uh," he said, and reached for her wrist, drawing her down beside him.

She nearly spilled her own drink, and he took it out of her hand and set it on the coffee table beside his own. His hand slid up her bare arm, holding her shoulder, and he kissed her.

She couldn't blame it on the scotch; she hadn't even sipped it yet. The tremor that ran through her was strictly from his touch, his nearness. Hunger rose inside her, and she felt it meet an answering hunger in his lips and the pressure of his arms.

Why hadn't she remembered it was like this, that a tiny flicker could build so quickly to a full-fledged conflagration? Kissing had been enough when she was an inexperienced kid, but now she knew what came after the first tentative caresses, and her body was winning out over her good intentions.

The only reason they didn't make it to the bedroom was that another light suddenly came on in the hallway and a small voice spoke.

"Mom? Are you here? I've got a sore throat."

Erin resurfaced reluctantly, feeling cheated. She was conscious of her mussed hair, and the undone buttons; confused, she wondered whether she'd undone them or Silas had.

He released her at once and she stood up, striving for a normal voice, as resentful at having been interrupted as she was relieved to have been reprieved at the last second.

"It really hurts, and I coughed and coughed," Sammie said. "I thought you'd hear me and bring some medicine."

"I'll get it," Erin assured her. "Climb back into bed."

Sammie glanced toward the living room, where only one small lamp was lighted. "Is someone here? Didn't Grandma go home yet?"

"Mr. Copetti's here. We came home from the movie and were sitting here talking," Erin said. The bright light in the bathroom seared her eyes as she searched the medicine cabinet for the right bottle.

"I didn't hear anybody talking," Sammie observed. "I thought you'd gone to bed and forgot the light."

Thank God she hadn't, Erin thought, pouring the liquid into a measured dropper. Imagine Sammie walking into the bedroom and finding them together. Erin would have been smothered in guilt. Sammie might even have told Ruth, and while it was really nobody's business but her own, she cringed from having Ruth know.

When she went back into the living room, feeling awkward and foolish, Silas stood watching her with a faint smile. "Kids. They're wonderful, aren't they?" he asked.

"I'm sorry," she said, and then added in a rush before she lost her nerve, because with returning sanity she realized it was important, "Silas, I really am sorry. I got carried away when I should have had more sense. I can't—can't get into something that I'm not willing to carry through on, and this was—impulse, bad judgment. If it weren't for Sammie—" She stopped, knowing she was making it worse, that she sounded adolescent and stupid, yet knowing at the same time that she was right.

She wouldn't have blamed him if he'd left in a huff. Instead, he grinned, bent to kiss her on the lips, and drew back.

"I know. I took advantage of you. Listen, I'll call you, all right?"

She listened to his retreating footsteps, muffled by the carpet in the hallway, and wondered if he really would. She couldn't blame him if he didn't, but the sense of loss was acute.

She turned off the light and then pushed aside the curtains to look out at him, watching as he got into his car and drove away.

After she'd gone to bed, Erin cried herself to sleep.

16.

Vonda Busby liked being a nurse. She had long since given up indulging in guilt feelings over the son she had abandoned to her parents. She had been little more than a child herself when the boy was born, and in no way prepared to take on the responsibility for another life. She couldn't even manage her own.

She had worked hard in nursing school, graduating with honors. Since then she'd held good jobs, made adequate salaries, and in general enjoyed her life.

She'd never married again. Nursing had toughened her up. She knew she could handle life, now, that she didn't need parents or a man to do it for her.

There had been men, of course. She wasn't so embittered by that early experience that she disliked men, or feared them. Not after she found out that she was desirable, that men would go to great lengths to impress her, to possess her.

Not that she'd ever really let any of them possess her. She didn't regard herself as promiscuous. There had not been a lot of affairs over the years, and she'd never gone to bed with anyone except when there had been mutual commitment, even though it was never the legal kind.

She'd never surrendered to any man purely for material benefit. Even old Henry Meldrum, age seventy, who had been her private patient for nearly eight months, had given her pleasure as well as material things. In fact, Henry had been one of her favorites. He was witty and sophisticated, and as trim as many younger men. If he hadn't had a heart attack and died just as he was recovering from an automobile accident, she might even have broken her own rule and married him. Henry had been *fun*.

She had not, as his stepsons angrily charged, used any undue influence on the old man so as to be remembered in his will. He could have found any number of pretty young things to sleep with him, for what he could pay. All he'd paid her was her salary, admittedly a good one, but hardly out of the ordinary.

She'd been moderately surprised at the size of the legacy, but not that she was listed among his heirs. She'd made a major contribution to his happiness in his final days, and Henry was a man who showed his gratitude.

She had consulted a stock broker who had been her patient after he had triple by-pass surgery and who seriously believed she'd saved his life. The inheritance was now invested in various stocks which would have enabled her to live without working, if she'd chosen to do so. When the dividends came in, they were invested in more stocks, diversified enough to provide some protection against the vagaries of the economy. She would take out enough to educate Loren and leave the rest intact until she needed the money in her old age.

A look in her mirror was enough to reassure her that old age was a long way off, but she'd seen enough to know that age came to everyone. When it came to her, it would be as comfortable as money could make it.

She was more amused than anything else by Matthew Brogan's determination to get her into his bed. There had been no man in her life since she'd taken the position of nursing supervisor at Forest Hills. She might easily have given in the first time he invited her to dinner one floor up from her own, except that it became a challenge. The old devil had told her straight out he didn't intend to get married again; she never told him that she wouldn't have married him if he'd asked her. Marriages were so messy when they ended. She liked her life neat and tidy, just the way it was.

Yet the game was intriguing. She had been no more surprised by the diamond-encrusted watch than she had been by Henry's legacy; she had accepted it with a smile, a rather cool kiss, and a simple "Thank you."

Not even the champagne that followed had gotten one stitch of clothes off her, though she had allowed him to kiss her more deeply than usual. Timed just before the night R.N. called her, as arranged, with an imaginary minor crisis, nothing that would call Brogan away with her.

She dressed for this evening's dinner with care, taking great pains with her makeup as well as choosing a long gown of a deep, electric blue that molded breasts and hips as if it were sprayed on. She knew what it could do to a man; she'd been wearing it the night Henry had his fatal heart attack.

She wore the diamond watch as her only jewelry. She had a hunch that something would be added to it before the evening was over. She hadn't decided yet whether or not she would at last stop tantalizing him, but as a safety measure she'd left instructions with Joan Warlum for a ten-thirty call. Joan was reliable, and without curiosity.

Vonda took the elevator upstairs, unconcerned about being seen. Five of the other R.N.s lived in the building, and the two doctors. By this time the nurses would either have gone out for the evening or have settled in with a book or TV, and Dr. Spaulding was so disassociated from real life that he'd attach no significance whatever to meeting her in an evening gown, going *up* to Dr. Brogan's floor.

She knew that Dr. Spaulding was brilliant, a fact hard to credit when one met him in person. She'd seen Lisa Brogan's picture and knew she'd been a beautiful young woman, and it was impossible to imagine her with Aaron Spaulding. If he weren't so unattractive, he might present an irresistible challenge, she thought.

Brogan was expansive, smiling, considerate. Freshly showered and shaved, wafting an expensive scent.

"Sit down, let me get you a drink," he said, moving toward the bar in one corner of the living room.

It was, of course, the nicest unit in the building. Professionally decorated in tones of beige and cream with a touch of rich brown and an occasional dab of scarlet. Lots of mirrors, so she could see her own reflection even when she was seated on the cream-colored sofa.

Vonda relaxed with the drink, content to enjoy the preliminaries. They wouldn't get to the main bout until after dinner had been served by the maid, who would then discreetly withdraw. There was a slight bulge in the left pocket of his suit coat, inviting more speculation than the bulge in his trousers.

Poor baby, she thought, further amused, and while he talked she considered the possibilities of the new gift.

It was a sapphire pendant surrounded by diamonds on a fine platinum chain, which he fastened around her neck with a clumsiness that caused his hand to brush her breast. She wondered how long he'd practiced that, so that it seemed genuinely awkward rather than intentional, no mean feat since the clasp was at the back of her neck. The old devil.

Yet both the pendant and the touch sent pleasurable tremors through her. When the phone rang, and he swore and answered it, then passed the receiver to her, Vonda had made up her mind.

"Ten-thirty," Joan Warlum said flatly.

"Oh, well, let him have another one, then," Vonda said. She hung up and smiled at the man watching her. "Mr. Denton. Poor thing, he's always hungry, but he's losing weight satisfactorily, so I thought an additional snack wouldn't be crucial."

"Maybe we should leave the receiver off the hook for a while," Matt Brogan said. "If there's a genuine emergency, they'll send one of the security men."

Vonda let her smile grow as she reached down and laid the receiver gently on the table.

She woke in darkness and knew at once that she was not in her own bed. For a few seconds Vonda lay flat, waiting for memory to return.

There was a muttered exclamation beside her, and she recognized Matthew Brogan's voice.

Ah, yes. She had finally allowed him to lure her into bed, and very nice it had been, too. She was almost sorry she'd wasted those other nights, when she could easily have been here earlier.

"Goddamn it, use your head!" Brogan suddenly said clearly, and one arm flailed out, so that he struck her on the breast.

Vonda rolled away from him, massaging the bruised area. Who was he talking to?

There were a few more words, badly garbled, then, "A bloody goddamned fortune!"

Umm. Interesting, Vonda thought, if it made any sense. She sat up on the edge of the bed, leaning forward to see the luminous dial of his alarm clock: 2:45. She hadn't meant to fall asleep. She'd much rather wake up in her own place in the morning.

She decided not to risk waking him by turning on a light; she slid off the bed and began to grope for her clothes, neatly folded over a chair. Passion was fine, but when you'd spent a month's salary on a dress, you didn't throw it on the floor.

"Listen," Brogan said, so clearly that she thought he'd awakened after all. "Dammit, listen."

No, he was still dreaming. The necklace, where had she left that? Now the dress. It had a back zipper, and three inches from the bottom, the damned thing stuck.

"Listen," Brogan said again. "Money, more money than either one of us ever thought of."

Some dream, Vonda thought. She jerked the zipper down, freeing it, then back up. Now where in hell were her shoes?

Brogan threw out a hand that brushed her backside as she bent over, groping over the carpet. This time his words were unintelligible.

Vonda found one sandal and swore. Where was the other one? She stretched an arm under the bed, and finally made contact with one of the thin silver straps.

Matthew Brogan was still muttering, though she couldn't understand it now. Quietly, in her bare feet, sandals dangling from one finger, she crossed the room and let herself out.

There was a dim glow in the living room from the glass tank where a dozen exotic fish swam lazily. Very effective as a nightlight, she thought. She'd get out of here without tripping over anything and waking up Dr. Brogan.

On the low table before the couch she saw two glasses, one of them still half full. He hadn't allowed her to finish it.

It was flat by now, of course, but she was thirsty. Vonda paused to drain the glass, then let herself out into the silent, carpeted corridor, and entered the elevator, which was still where she'd left it.

In the dark bedroom behind her, Matthew Brogan said, "I knew I could persuade you to be sensible," before he fell back into dreamless sleep.

17.

Paula Lundstrom stood at the foot of his bed when he opened his eyes, an uncertain smile flickering on her face. "Hi, Daddy."

Ernie Denton stared at her but said nothing.

"I thought you'd be up and around this time of day," Paula said nervously. "Mrs. Randall told me you'd been down for breakfast."

"I'm tired," the old man said stolidly. "Can't a man take a nap in peace?"

"I didn't wake you, did I? I'd been standing here for several minutes . . ."

"Where's my wallet?"

Disconcerted, Paula allowed her jaw to sag momentarily. "Your wallet? What do you need a wallet for, Daddy? I'm writing checks for the bills."

"A man don't feel like a man without his wallet. A little money, pictures, identification. That kind of thing."

Comprehension washed over her. "Oh, you want a picture of Mama? I can bring you that nice silver-framed one that's in the den, if you'd like it."

"I don't want that one. I want my wallet, goddamn it. Would that be too much to ask?"

Paula swallowed. "No, of course not. I'll bring it next time I come."

"Tonight," Ernie said. "Bring it tonight."

"Yes, of course," Paula agreed. "Is there anything else I can bring you?"

"Chocolates. A box of those creams from See's. Not the mixture, just the soft ones. I can't chew the goddamned hard ones anymore."

"Daddy, you know you're supposed to be losing weight."

"What the hell difference does it make, at this stage of things? I *am* losing weight, in case you haven't noticed! Goddamned clothes falling right off me! Tell 'em to put in plenty of raspberry creams."

He was grateful that she didn't stay, trying to make conversation. They'd run out of things to say to each other years ago. She didn't really want to hear how he felt, or what he thought about anything. All she wanted was to have him out of her house, away from her guests, so his fat and his table manners wouldn't embarrass her.

He thought about getting out of bed and going down to the basement to his trains after she'd left, but he really was tired. Running down, he thought. Like an old clock, nobody winding it anymore, and pretty soon it was going to quit.

The idea no longer frightened him; he'd had plenty of time to think about it and had decided that even if there wasn't any afterlife, it didn't matter. *This* life sure didn't have a hell of a lot left to offer him. What did bother him was having to die here, and not being allowed to have the food that offered the only pleasure left to him until it happened.

"Okay if I clean in here?"

He hadn't even noticed her, standing there in the doorway with her cart full of buckets and cleaning supplies. Mrs. Baczewski. She was a scrawny old thing. She wore old, much-polished white shoes with a seam split in the left one to accommodate a bunion.

She was a garrulous creature, though he'd made it clear the first time she came that he didn't care to listen. It wasn't his duty to entertain the help while they did their chores, was it? He'd often heard her in the room across the hall, or in other rooms when he was passing by, talking about her children (she had six) or her grandchildren (there were fourteen) and her husband, who still drove a truck at the age of sixty. Although he didn't let her talk to him, Ernie knew all about her gallbladder operation and her sister-in-law who lived in Phoenix with two palm trees in her front yard. Who the hell cared about palm trees? They were messy and didn't make any shade.

"I guess if you don't answer, it means it won't bother you," she said, and moved the cart into the room.

Ernie's eyes followed her as she wiped down various surfaces with a rag, vacuumed, disinfected. Mrs. Baczewski hummed and talked to herself. "Well, now, what got spilled here?" Or "Oh, oh, that bulb's burned out. Have to bring you a new one." He thought she did it mainly to annoy him.

Another thing that annoyed him was the jangling of the great ring of keys she carried, removing it from her belt when she had to gain access to one of the locked cupboards of supplies. Locked, by God, as if the patients were going to steal the toilet paper.

The keys, Ernie thought. She was a stupid woman. It ought to be possible to get the keys.

Nobody asked about the keys until late afternoon. Then Janet stuck her head around the doorframe to inquire, "You didn't see a bunch of keys, did you?"

He gave her his customary baleful stare, wordless.

"Mrs. Baczewski's misplaced hers somewhere. She must have dropped them."

He still didn't answer and Janet gave him a grin. "You want to go downstairs for dinner? It's prime rib. I think there's cherry pie for dessert."

"I'm perfectly capable of going down to dinner," he said with dignity. "Shut the door now. I want to take a nap."

"Good. I'll take you down in forty-five minutes," Janet promised, and was gone.

Alone behind the closed door, Ernie took out the keys—very carefully, so as to keep them quiet—and examined them. As he had hoped, they were labeled. And as he had prayed, there was one marked FRONT DOOR.

He sighed and tried to recall what he'd learned about the schedules of the security guards.

Paula Lundstrom paused before the open doorway of Dr. Brogan's office on her way out. He looked up and smiled, then rose to his feet.

"Come in, Mrs. Lundstrom. Is there something I can do for you?"

She stepped inside, twisting at a button on her jacket without realizing that she did it. "It's . . . how is my father doing, Doctor?"

He waved her toward a chair so that he could resume his own seat. "I'd say his progress is satisfactory. He hasn't come around to liking us, yet, and his complaints continue." He smiled ruefully. "Mostly about the food. You've seen our menus, and our trays, so you know how much justification he has."

"Yes. The food is . . . marvelous. I'm sorry he's so unreasonable—"

"No, no, no need to apologize for him. Our staff knows how to handle that sort of thing. Physically, I'm pleased with his improvement. He's lost twenty-two pounds, and he's a bit more active. Spent two hours in the basement with his trains yesterday."

Paula hesitated, then blurted out her concern. "I can see he's lost weight. Twenty-two pounds is rather a lot, isn't it, in such a short time? It—it isn't dangerous to lose so fast, is it?"

"No, no. We monitor his condition carefully. Of course there is a little loose skin, that's to be expected, but every pound off reduces the stress on his heart and lungs."

"He—I almost hesitate to say this, but he's demanding that I bring him a box of candy."

"Is he? Well, bring it in and give it to the nurse in charge. We'll let him have his little treat in measured doses."

Paula exhaled in relief and rose from her chair. "Thank you, Doctor. I feel much better about him now."

He rose to escort her to the door. "Anytime that anything bothers you, just drop in and talk about it. We're trying to take very good care of your father, you know."

"Yes, I do know. And I'm very grateful," Paula told him. She had been so lucky, she told herself on her way out to her car, to find a place like Forest Hills.

18.

Four days had passed, and Silas hadn't called. Erin alternated between genuine regret—she liked him very much—and anger.

Did she want a man who expected her to go to bed with him at once? (It had really been a first date; the excursions with the kids didn't count.) Maybe that was the way everybody else did it these days; she'd been out of the dating game for so long that her ideas were archaic.

In her rational moments, though—which included practically all of them, except for those when she crawled, alone, into the big bed—she knew that her decision was the only sensible one. Sammie was at an impressionable age; if there was an affair, she was certainly sharp enough to be aware of it. So which was more important, Erin asked herself, easing her own physical urges, or raising a daughter with the moral standards she wanted the child to have?

It was no contest, yet the ache and the resentment lingered.

On Friday night, just before time to lock up her desk and head for home, an ambulance pulled up before the front door.

Erin stood up, glancing at her appointment book, though she knew there were no scheduled new arrivals due. The security guard moved to open the double doors, admitting the ambulance attendants with the guerney; they were followed by several women and a man who seemed vaguely familiar.

It was not until she looked down at the face of the patient strapped onto the guerney that Erin identified the trio: the son and two daughters of Mrs. Tosta, for the patient was Mrs. Tosta herself.

Shock held Erin rigid for a moment. The woman was so wasted that recognition had not been instantaneous.

It was the man who spoke. "I don't know if we did right, bringing her here instead of to the regular hospital, but she thinks so much of Dr. Brogan. This is where she wanted to come."

"She collapsed, half an hour ago," one of the daughters contributed. Her face was creased with anxiety. "She hasn't been doing real well, anyway, she's sort of gone downhill ever since we took her home, but today—" Her voice broke, and she fumbled for a handkerchief.

"Where do you want her?" an attendant asked, and Erin recovered her wits.

"Just a moment, please. We weren't expecting her, so I'll have to check with the nurse, or Dr. Brogan."

A call to Brogan's office was answered immediately. "Yes?"

Erin relayed the information as succinctly as she could. With the relatives standing right there, and Mrs. Tosta possibly able to hear even though she appeared comatose, she couldn't express her own shock at the old woman's appearance.

Brogan said, "I'll be right there. And call Miss Busby, too, will you, please?"

It was out of Erin's hands after that, but she stayed late while the son filled out the admittance papers and Mrs. Tosta was taken away upstairs. Brogan's countenance had revealed nothing but professional concern as he bent over the guerney, yet Erin had seen Vonda Busby flinch when she looked into the emaciated face of the old woman who had left here so blithely such a short time ago.

"You want to keep her here, or shall we take her on to General?" one of the ambulance attendants asked, obviously wanting to leave.

Dr. Brogan didn't reply directly. "Have her transferred to one of our own guerneys, Miss Busby, and we'll admit her." And then, to the relatives, "We'll probably keep her overnight, at least, to give us time to evaluate her condition. If it merits intensive care, we will have to transfer her, of course; we're not set up for that here at Forest Hills, as you know."

"Of course. She'd much rather be here, if it's possible," the son said.

Mrs. Tosta was removed, the staff went with her, the relatives and the ambulance crew departed. Erin put on her coat and nodded to the security man, who opened the door for her to leave.

Maybe she'd overestimated her own ability to deal with tragedy, she thought, sliding into her car. Mrs. Tosta had looked so well, leaving here only a few weeks ago, and now she appeared to be dying. Erin shivered in the cold and turned on the heater full blast.

She stopped at Ruth's to pick up Sammie, listening to the child's chatter with half an ear on the way home, then stood staring without enthusiasm into the refrigerator.

"Let's have toasted cheese sandwiches and tomato soup," Sammie suggested.

"You had that only night before last," Erin reminded, though she was already beginning to weaken. "What did you have for lunch at school?"

"Spaghetti and meat balls. With carrot strips and canned peaches. Please, Mom, let's have toasted cheese."

The telephone rang before Erin could reply. Sammie reached it first, then handed it over with a grin. "It's Mr. Copetti. If you go out with him, can I have toasted cheese?"

She hadn't, of course, bothered to put a hand over the receiver, so he'd heard that. Erin felt her cheeks burn as she spoke into the phone. "Hi."

His voice sounded friendly, not put off by Sammie's suggestion that he might invite her out, whether or not that was his intention. Of course he had a seven-year-old of his own, so he knew how blunt they could be.

"Hi. Sorry it took me so long to get back to you, I've been out of town for a few days on a case. It earned me a nice fee, and I wondered if you'd like to help me spend it. Say, dinner, a few drinks, some conversation."

"It sounds like fun," Erin admitted, unable to quell the elation she felt just in hearing his voice. "Only my baby-sitter is going out with a friend to celebrate a birthday tonight. I don't know anybody else to ask; Sammie's always stayed with her grandmother when she couldn't be with me."

"How about if I pick up something and come over there, then?" Silas asked. "Do you like Chinese?"

"I love Chinese."

"Give me forty-five minutes," he said, and the line went dead.

"Are you going out?" Sammie asked hopefully.

"No, didn't you just hear me say Grandma can't keep you tonight? But you can have your toasted cheese and soup while I take a shower, and then you can move the TV into your room to watch until bedtime while Silas and I sit in the living room with our own dinner, okay?"

She was glad he was coming. She wanted something pleasant to think about, not dying old people. By the time she was ready in a soft green wool dress with the jade pendant that Ted had given her on their first anniversary, she'd almost managed to put Mrs. Tosta out of her mind.

Silas took it for granted that he'd help her clean up after the meal, stowing all the remains of pork fried rice and sweet and sour pork and exotic vegetables and chicken in her refrigerator, loading their dishes into the dishwasher.

"I'm going to have to get myself one of these things," he said, closing the door. "I hate dirty dishes in the sink, but it seems stupid to fix hot water and suds for one plate and one glass."

"I know. It's one of the advantages of this place. What kind of music shall I put on?"

He stood close beside her, looking over the tapes, and she let him choose: dreamy, romantic music.

"I haven't danced in a long time," he said, and drew her into his arms.

It wasn't possible, Erin thought, that she could feel so strongly that she belonged there. She and Ted had dated for months before she'd really felt that way with him; it had taken them nearly a year to decide to get married, and there hadn't been any sex until after the wedding.

Even later, when Sammie had been sent to take her bath, and then on to bed, when they sat on the couch and talked and held hands before they got around to kissing, Erin wondered at herself. Was she just sex-starved or did she really care about this man so much?

"You know," Silas murmured into her hair, "it isn't going to be easy, playing by your rules. What would you think of changing them, if we adjusted the basic game?"

Erin drew back enough to look into his face. "What's that supposed to mean?"

"Well, up to now we've been getting acquainted. Say we move

on to 'engagement,' like 'getting married in the spring, or maybe sooner,' and see where that takes us."

For an instant she froze. Was it simply a ploy to take them to bed, or was he serious?

"I'm not sure I'm ready for a change in the rules," she said, feeling idiotic that she sounded so prim, so old-fashioned, so . . . so *stuffy*.

"And I thought my charm was winning you over." The soft words brought his breath against her cheek, and then his mouth covered hers, deceptively gentle at first, the building passion sneaking up on her.

His hands—she liked his hands—had somehow strayed from the back of her neck and her shoulder to the curves of thigh and breast. Even though they were both fully dressed, Erin felt enveloped in heat.

She heard a groan—his or hers?—and then the moment was shattered as the telephone rang.

"Dammit, did you plan that?" Silas asked as she withdrew from him.

Erin scarcely heard. It was a quarter past eleven; who'd be calling at this hour? Ruth—Ruth had been out tonight, and it was a rainy, nasty evening. Had there been an accident?

The voice that answered her breathless "Yes?" was familiar, though it didn't belong to her mother-in-law. Vonda Busby spoke crisply.

"Erin? Sorry to bother you so late, but we have an emergency on our hands."

"It's okay, I was still up. What's happened?" She searched her mind, frantic, for anything she might have done to contribute to an emergency.

"Mr. Denton's missing."

It took a few seconds for that to soak in. "Missing?" Erin echoed stupidly. "How . . . ?"

"We think he swiped Mrs. Baczewski's keys. She noticed this afternoon that they were gone, and she couldn't remember exactly where she had them last, but thinks it may have been in Mr. Denton's room. He demanded that his daughter bring him his wallet, which she did during evening visiting hours. She thinks it had only about fifty dollars in it, but it was loaded with credit cards.

To add to that, we found some papers in his room that seem to be a record of where the staff members are at any given time, including the security force. The consensus here is that the old man walked out the front door after using Mrs. Baczewski's keys at a time when the security men were away from the front of the building. The gates are closed at night, but they aren't locked."

"I—I wouldn't have thought he could walk very far," Erin said, as much relieved that none of this could be laid to her account as alarmed for the old man. "He puffs so just walking across the room . . ."

"Yes, well, the security men have combed the grounds, and he's gone beyond our own boundaries, anyway."

"Have you notified the police?" Erin turned to look back into the living room, and saw Silas pause in the act of lighting a cigarette.

"Not yet. We're probably going to have to, but we'd rather not have that sort of publicity," Vonda told her. "First we're checking with all the staff members to see if anyone can think of anything he's done or said that would give us a few clues. We haven't even notified his daughter yet; Dr. Brogan says we'll use the excuse that he disappeared so late that we didn't want to disturb her, but we'll have to call her first thing in the morning, whether or not he's found. I know you haven't talked to him much, nobody has, except Janet; she can't think of a thing he's said that hinted at running away, but she's convinced he won't go to his daughter's place. He seems very hostile toward the Lundstroms."

Silas had risen from the couch and came toward her, smoke forgotten. He waited, eyes holding hers, as Erin said, "I can't think of a thing. He has only one theme, really—he's always complaining that he doesn't get enough to eat. He's obsessed with food."

"Yes. Well, possibly this explains the supplies that have been missing from the kitchen. Nothing major, but the cooks have complained. Janet suggested Mr. Denton might have stolen them, but we really didn't think he could have managed to get down there by himself, undetected. If you think of anything else, though, call us, will you? No matter what time it is?"

"Yes, of course. Good night, then."

She replaced the receiver and stood thinking this over until Silas said, "Somebody escaped from the marvelous hospital?"

She felt a twinge of resentment at the seemingly facetious remark.

"One of the patients, a Mr. Denton, apparently appropriated the cleaning woman's keys and just walked out tonight."

"*Do* they starve him?" Silas wanted to know.

"No, of course not. He's on a reducing diet, he came in weighing about three hundred pounds, but he certainly isn't being starved. I've seen some of his meals, and they're fantastic. In fact, I don't even know how he's lost all that weight on his 'diet.' *I'd* gain on that kind of meal."

Silas regarded her thoughtfully. "How do they manage that?"

She replied absently, thinking how the Lundstroms were going to react to the news that the old man had disappeared when the hospital was being paid a small fortune to look after him. "I don't know. Mrs. Tosta had lost quite a bit too; she looked great when she left a few weeks ago. Only tonight when they brought her back in she was almost like . . . like a cadaver."

"She kept on losing after she went home, and then had to come back?"

"Yes, she collapsed at home—" She stopped, staring at him. There was something in his voice, a subdued intensity, that suggested he was doing more than making small talk about a situation that was of no real interest to him.

"Did you know Sylvia Miller was fat when she went to work at Forest Hills?"

Erin felt her jaw dropping, and snapped her mouth shut. "Sylvia? *Fat?*"

Before it had quite registered that he knew Sylvia, Silas added a bomb shell.

"Did you know that was what she quarreled with her boyfriend about, just before she killed herself? That she was getting too skinny, and he wanted her to stop reducing?"

Erin felt as if she'd stepped off a train in a strange place, where there wasn't enough light so that she could orient herself. She had two worlds—home and work—and now Silas had moved beyond home into work, and he didn't belong there.

She had forgotten Ernie Denton.

"How do you know Sylvia?" she asked.

19.

Ten minutes later they still stood confronting one another in Erin's living room. He had explained—yet there was so much that remained unexplained.

She understood his concern about his uncle, who had died at Forest Hills before she went there. She didn't understand at all why he was perturbed about Sylvia Miller.

"Because," Silas said patiently, "she worked there, and *she* died too. Only she wasn't old and sick, she was young and pretty and she was engaged to be married. She shouldn't have killed herself, but she did."

"She *was* upset about something, the day before. I found her crying in the rest room," Erin admitted. "She'd had a fight with her fiancé. People have killed themselves before, over lovers' quarrels."

"Over a matter of the girl's weight, for crissake?" He sounded a little less patient than he had been before. "She was quite plump when her boyfriend met her, and he was pleased at how pretty she was when she slimmed down. But he thought she was getting too skinny, which she was; the day she rode in my cab, she was wearing a suit that practically fell off her. He wanted her to stop dieting. Is that something a normally sensible girl would kill herself over?"

"How do you know what he wanted, or what he said to her?"

"I asked him. I went to his house the night it happened. He was bewildered, feeling guilty without knowing why."

"Why?" Erin demanded.

"Why, what?"

"Why did you go to his house? You didn't really know Sylvia."

"She was a young girl with everything to live for, and she killed herself. She worked at the place where my Uncle Isadore died, and my aunt didn't think he should have died, either, even though he was getting on in years. I wanted to know if there was a reason, for either of them."

"And what about me?" she asked, fighting the inward quaking that threatened to become obvious.

"What about you?"

"Was it all a setup? The picnic in the park, the zoo, then asking us both for an outing on the beach? You asked a lot of questions about my job, about Dr. Brogan and the others. Was that why you picked me up, because I worked at Forest Hills and you wanted to use me to find out what you wanted to know?"

He deliberately lighted the cigarette this time, blowing smoke before he answered. His dark eyes sent a shiver down her back; he must have looked this way at the criminals he'd arrested when he was a cop.

"I haven't found out a hell of lot yet, have I? Lady, I ran into you quite accidentally at the deli, and I'd already promised Patty a picnic in the park. Sure, I knew you worked at Forest Hills. At least, I knew you had some connection there, I saw you leaving the place. You had the best-looking legs I ever saw short of Las Vegas, and given the opportunity I'd have picked you up anywhere. Does that mean I should ignore the fact that you might be a source of information in a case I'm interested in?"

"Is there a case? Are you working for someone, investigating Forest Hills?"

"I'm doing my Aunt Tillie a favor, and I'm satisfying my own curiosity. There's something damned funny about that place, and I want to know what it is. If that bothers you, I'm sorry, but I was a cop for too many years to be able to see a puzzle without wanting to solve it, whether I'm working for anybody for a fee or not."

"But I've told you there's nothing 'funny' about Forest Hills! It's a marvelous place to work, a marvelous place for people who are old and sick!"

"And Dr. Brogan should be elevated to sainthood because he's absolutely perfect. I don't believe it, Erin. He has no flaws at all, and that makes him only the second such man in two thousand years. Bullshit!"

She stared at him in helpless exasperation. "I never said he didn't have any flaws. He has two divorced wives who would know better than I would. All I said was that he's wonderful to work for, kind and considerate of his help, caring and competent with his patients. That doesn't mean he's a closet ogre or something, does it?"

Disconcertingly, Silas laughed.

"Now what?" Erin asked, annoyed.

"You think he's great, so why don't you help me clear him?"

"Clear him? Of what, for God's sake? What are you accusing him of? What's anybody accusing him of?"

"I don't know for sure, but there's something there." His amusement had vanished. "You hear any talk about a woman used to work there, a Mrs. Masterson? Died recently?"

"Yes, she was a bookkeeper. She had to retire when she suffered a stroke. What's she got to do with anything?"

"Well, she died. At age fifty-six. People *do* die at that age, but it's pretty young. Has anybody mentioned Mrs. Masterson?"

"I was there when Dr. Brogan read her obituary in the paper. He was deeply sorry about it, that's all."

"Nobody else mentioned her?"

"Only Sylvia." She didn't try to check the defensive note in her voice. "She liked Mrs. Masterson—I gather they all did—and Sylvia said she was the only other one of the original help who'd left—the bookkeeper because of the stroke, and Sylvia was leaving to get married."

Silas took a drag on the cigarette and ground it out in the nearest ashtray. "Only Sylvia didn't get married, and they both died."

"People die all the time! You're making a mountain out of a mole hill! You're paranoid!"

"I think multiple deaths might be considered something bigger than a mole hill, and you're damned right I'm paranoid. I've got a gut instinct that tells me there is something so fishy at that place that I can smell it a mile away, and I want to know what it is. You could help me, Erin. You're in the place. You could tell me what goes on."

"*Nothing* goes on, except that sick people are taken care of and made comfortable! Go visit some of the patients, talk to *them!* They'll all tell you, they love it there!"

"Except Mr. Denton, who ran away."

"Mr. Denton is a nasty, disagreeable old man who doesn't love anyone or anything. Not even himself."

"Sylvia Miller wasn't old or disagreeable. An ex-fat girl who couldn't stand it when her boyfriend wanted her to stop dieting. It doesn't make sense."

He must have caught the flicker of expression change on her face, for he reached out and clamped a hand on her shoulder. "What is it? What did you remember?"

Erin moistened her lips and spoke reluctantly. "Sylvia. She wasn't dieting. Not the whole time she worked with me. We ate all our meals together at the hospital, and she wasn't on a diet at all."

His eyes narrowed. "You're sure?"

"Well, she didn't appear to be. At coffee break she'd eat cinnamon rolls with butter on them, or whatever the treat was. There's always something home-baked. Most of the staff, the single ones, anyway, eat their main meal of the day at noon, because that's when the big meals are cooked. Dr. Brogan thinks it's better than a heavy meal at night. I . . . I do it too, and so did Sylvia. Baked potatoes and sour cream, chops or steaks or prime rib, rich desserts. I've even stopped having breakfast at home, so I dare eat what I want later on, at the hospital."

"Only Sylvia didn't seem to be worrying about eating too much."

"No," Erin said reluctantly.

He dropped his hand from her shoulder. "How about this Mrs. Masterson? Was *she* dieting? Fat, skinny, what?"

"I don't know. She was gone before I got there."

"You could find out," Silas suggested softly.

"What difference does it make?" Erin asked, but she wasn't quite able to work up to her previous level of indignation.

"I don't know, but I'll make you a bet. I'll bet she was fat, at least when she started work there. And that she wasn't fat at all when she died."

"Well, that's possible. One of the things Dr. Brogan seems successful with is weight loss in obese patients. He likes his staff to be attractive, so I suppose he'd help them lose weight too if they needed to."

He sounded suddenly tired. "So far all we have is another piece of the puzzle, but I think it may be a key one, even if I don't know what it means. Why didn't Sylvia stop losing weight, if she wasn't dieting anymore? Find out about Mrs. Masterson, at least. See if she was ever fat."

"You're asking me to spy on people who've been very good to me," Erin said slowly. "To dig into things that are none of my business."

"If any of these people didn't die a natural death—and Sylvia sure as hell didn't—then it's everybody's business, isn't it? If they're all as simon-pure as you think, nothing you look into is going to hurt them, is it?"

Though she still didn't like it, there was a certain logic in what he said. She was convinced he was wrong, that there were reasonable explanations for all his questions. And she wouldn't begin to know how to spy, anyway.

He took her silence for acquiescence. "There's just one thing, Erin. Be careful about making inquiries. If there *is* something fishy there, getting curious could be dangerous."

He grinned then, and became Silas the man rather than Silas the cop. "We seem to be ill-fated, don't we? Between kids and telephone calls, we're never allowed to follow through on anything. I'll call you tomorrow, okay?"

He didn't kiss her good night. Erin locked the door behind him. She thought he was completely off base regarding Forest Hills and Dr. Brogan, yet it *was* curious about Sylvia. What was he suggesting, that Dr. Brogan had somehow driven Sylvia to suicide? Impossible. And Brogan's shock and concern had been genuine, she was sure of it.

Silas hadn't gotten back to the subject of themselves. It had sounded like a proposal of marriage, and she didn't know how she felt about that. If this other business hadn't come up, how would she have reacted?

She liked him a lot, but she wasn't sure if she loved him.

She had felt so close to him before Vonda Busby had called. It had been such a lovely evening. And now she had to go to bed wondering if he'd sought her out for herself or because he wanted to use her in an investigation.

Damn Silas Copetti anyway, she thought angrily, and turned out the lights and went to bed.

20.

It was both easier and more difficult than he'd expected.

The cleaning woman's keys let him out of the front door, and he had sense enough to know that he should lock it behind him; otherwise, the security men would discover that it was open and the alarm would go out too soon.

Ernie Denton stepped into the chill, wet night. There were lights near the gates, and he was worried about that because he could see that they were closed, and he had no key on his ring labeled GATES.

There were lights on posts along the sidewalk and parking area too; light reflected in the puddles on the paving and on the hoods of the cars. He stood for a moment, shivering, listening. The security men should be, at this time, one checking the back of the building, the other over at the laboratory. He drew a wavering breath and stepped out along the ramp that led to the parking lot.

This was where it got easier. The first car he came to showed the glint of keys dangling from the ignition. Careless, even for someone trusting to security guards, but fine for his purposes.

He hadn't driven a car in years. He couldn't remember how many. But driving a car was easy these days; all you had to do was turn on the key and steer the goddamned thing.

It wasn't a big, new, or fancy car. Belonged to one of the night-shift aides, no doubt. Ernie tried to slide in behind the wheel and found it impossible; he fumbled around until he located the lever that allowed the seat to be moved backward to make the maximum amount of space between his body and the wheel, and even then he just barely squeezed into it.

He didn't know if the sound of the motor starting would alert the guards or not. It was too early for any of the staff to be going home. Again luck was with him, though; the motor purred to life, smooth and well-lubricated.

Ernie squinted to see where to shift it into reverse, and the car jolted backward; he only barely managed to hit the brake before he crashed into another car. Jesus, that would bring the security men running, he thought. He was sweating now, in spite of the chill.

He shifted into drive and began to ease the car down the gentle slope toward the front gates. He had to get out of the car there, and the miracle held: the tall wrought-iron sections came open easily and he drove through, stopping with the car blocking one lane of the street while he reclosed the gates. He was wheezing rather badly by the time he climbed back in and headed the car toward town.

Nothing looked the same as he remembered it. He knew his own house—his son-in-law's house, now—was not far, but he couldn't exactly remember where. It didn't matter; he didn't want to go there, anyway.

Where he did want to go was some cheap hotel, one where he could hole up and be safe. Oh, he knew they'd find him eventually, unless he kept moving around, because they'd trace the credit cards. He wished he had more cash, they couldn't trace *that*.

Oncoming cars kept blinking their lights at him. It wasn't until a horn blared that he realized he hadn't turned on the headlights. Where was the knob for that, anyway? He nearly ran up onto the curb trying to find it, and his breathing was worse by the time he pulled the knob and hoped he'd pulled the right one. He couldn't tell by the amount of light ahead of the car.

Where was the district where the cheap hotels were? He was confused, disoriented, because there were all kinds of buildings and signs he didn't remember ever having seen before. He *was* still in San Cristobal, wasn't he?

He was in the business district now. Surely there'd be something he'd recognize; he'd run his own store here for nearly sixty years. Ah, there, the bank, his own bank . . .

He scraped a parking meter and climbed the curb before he could bring his metal steed to a halt. Yes, his headlights were on; they clearly illuminated the cash machine beside the double doors.

Of course, how could he have forgotten? He had a card, somewhere, if Paula hadn't removed it from his wallet.

It took him a few minutes to extricate himself from the driver's seat. God, he was tired! He flipped through the credit cards until he found the right one, and carried it over and stuck it in the slot. And sure enough, the money came out. Two hundred dollars.

He crammed the bills in with the others, and got back in the car. Now, if this was the bank, and across the street was the Rexall Drug, then the cheap hotels ought to be over that way.

He backed off the curb with a crunching sound, shot across the street and glanced off a parked van, and veered onto the side street before anyone appeared to check the damage.

He was drenched in rancid perspiration, and his breathing was so loud he couldn't hear anything else. He drove for several minutes without awareness of where he was, or that other cars swerved to avoid his, thinking only of how bad he sounded. When he returned to consciousness of his surroundings, he saw the sign for the motel.

Yes, better than a hotel. He swung the wheel sharply, then had to correct quickly to avoid crashing into the side of the building next door. He rested for a moment before he had the strength to turn off the ignition and get out.

The young man in the office, reading *Hustler*, looked up with a bored expression. He was about twenty-two; he had bad skin and a catsup stain on his tie.

"Yeah?" he said.

Ernie Denton pulled out his wallet. "You take credit cards?"

"Yeah. Visa, Master Charge, American Express. You want a room?"

"What else would I want?" Ernie asked, fishing out a Visa card with trembling fingers. "There an all-night restaurant close by?"

"There's a Denny's two blocks over, on Santa Rosa." The young man pushed a registration form toward him, along with a pen.

Ernie stared at it helplessly. He wasn't sure how long his legs would hold him up. "You fill it out. Name's on the card."

The fellow looked at him. "You sick?"

"I've felt better," Ernie admitted. "Hurry up, will you?"

The youth shrugged and copied his name off the card. "Where you from? Home address?"

For a moment he couldn't think at all. This was San Cristobal, but if he told him that, the fellow would wonder why he didn't go home. He might even call there.

"San Francisco," he said. He made up an address. "Twelve-ten Dolbeer Street." Was there a Dolbeer Street in San Francisco? Or was that only in Eureka? He was *sure* there was one in Eureka.

The clerk wrote it down without comment. "Just the one night, sir?"

"I don't know. Probably several nights," Ernie said.

"License number?"

Ernie stared at him blankly.

"License number," the clerk repeated. "You know, car license."

A number floated into his memory. "MJB 723." It was from a very old car, one he'd had when Paula was a child. She'd memorized it and chanted it like a little song.

"Okay. Here you are. Number fourteen, straight back." He slid a key with a large yellow plastic tag attached to it across the counter.

Ernie went out into the drizzle. He was starving, but he didn't know if he could drive another few blocks to the Denny's. He wanted very badly to lie down and rest. A door opened beside him and a young couple came out. The girl was laughingly protesting.

"I'm not hungry enough to walk that far in the rain for a hamburger," she said.

"You want me to walk it by myself? While you pick up another guy when I'm gone?"

Ernie Denton cleared his throat. "Excuse me. You going to Denny's for something to eat?"

They stared at him uncertainly. They were very young, and the girl was pretty in a cheap, skinny way.

"Yeah, maybe," the boy said at last.

Ernie scrabbled for his wallet, found it in the pocket of his jacket. He whipped out several bills. "Here. Take this, take my car. Keys are in it, right there. Bring me back something to eat."

They exchanged glances, and the girl said, "Why not?"

"Okay. What room you in?"

He tried to think, and couldn't remember; the girl reached out and turned over the yellow tag on his key. "Fourteen," she said. "Room fourteen."

The boy was staring at the money. "What do you want to eat?"

Ernie scraped his memory for a clue as to what was available at Denny's. "Reubens. Patty-melts. French fries. Chocolate shakes."

"All of them?" the boy asked, incredulous.

"Whatever that'll buy. Anything, just bring me a lot of food."

"Fifty dollars worth?"

"Yes, and hurry. Hurry," he said.

He heard their excited voices behind him but, paid them no attention. The key turned in the lock, letting him into warmth and the smell of old cigars and cheap booze. There was a worn orange spread on the slightly sagging bed; he didn't notice. It felt so good to lie down, though he had to put the pillows together so he wouldn't be flat. It was so hard to breathe when he was flat.

Gradually the wheezing subsided; he thought he might even have slept a few minutes when the boy rapped on the door.

He had to get up to admit them, standing to one side while they carried in the boxes of food and placed them on the dresser. The boy handed him some silver. "Here's your change. I parked the car right in front of your door."

He remembered, then. He mustn't be connected with the car. They'd know he'd taken it, they'd trace him through it.

"Wait," he said. This time he brought out a ten-dollar bill. "You take the car back for me. I'll pay you."

The kids exchanged glances. "Where you want me to take it?" the boy asked.

"To—to—" He couldn't think of an address. He couldn't even remember his own address. How could he forget where he'd lived for forty years?

And then the memory of the name, read backward over the gates, though he'd read it forward when they brought him in. "Forest Hills," he said. "It's a hospital out—" But he couldn't remember the street.

"I know where it is," the girl said. "Do we just leave it in the parking lot, or turn the keys over to somebody, or what?"

"No, no, park it on the street, leave the keys in it."

The boy stared at the ten. "Well, I guess we could take a bus back here. The buses are still running, aren't they? Or a cab. Okay, mister, it's your car, we'll leave the keys in it."

He was glad when they were gone. He sat on the edge of the bed and ate two patty-melts and a Reuben, and drank two chocolate shakes. Then he crawled into the bed, fully clothed, and listened to his breathing in the dark.

He wondered how long it would be before the clock stopped.

21.

The day was as bad as Erin expected.

She knew the moment she walked through the front doors and saw Janet, the aide, that they hadn't found Mr. Denton.

"Apparently he stole Jinny's car and it's all smashed up. Looks like he ran into everything he got near."

"Where did they find the car? He couldn't have gone far on his own, not when he couldn't walk the length of the hallway," Erin said, hanging up her coat. "Did they get any clues from that?"

"No. The car was parked in front of the hospital with the keys in it. Nobody knows how it got back here, and nobody knows where to look for him. He must have walked somewhere on his own. Jinny's in hysterics about her car, it isn't paid for, and Tom says it'll probably take twelve or fifteen hundred dollars worth of bodywork."

"Have they notified his daughter yet?"

"Dr. Brogan's talking to her on the phone now." Janet cast an apprehensive glance along the corridor. "Everybody's afraid to go near his office."

"Was he very angry?"

"Furious," Janet asserted. "He and Miss Busby had some rather harsh words, though I can't see that it's her fault any more than anyone else's, and she wasn't on duty. The old man was sly, and a sneak. He's been getting downstairs to the kitchen at night. You wouldn't believe the crap they found in his dresser drawers—crumbs, and peelings, and chop bones, and a mouse feeding on a stale roll. If anything, Mrs. Baczewski should be blamed for not paying more attention to her keys. *Now* she's sure she dropped them in his room, but she wasn't sure last night. If she'd figured that out before she went home, maybe somebody would have caught him with them before he got away."

Erin drew a deep breath. "Well, I suppose I'd better check in with Dr. Brogan and see what he wants me to do. I wonder if they'll call the police."

"Everybody thinks it would be crazy to call them, terrible publicity for the place. But how else are they going to find him? He might be senile—at least he forgets a lot of things—but he's really rather clever about getting his own way. He was mad when Warlum wouldn't let him keep the box of chocolates his daughter brought in last night; she allowed him four of them, and said she'd keep the rest at her desk, and somehow he managed to swipe them during the evening visiting hours. We found the little cups they come in on the floor in his room. I guess he ate the whole two pounds."

The elevator doors opened as they approached and Vonda Busby got out. She was trim and professional in her white uniform and the black-banded cap with the gold pin from her nursing school on one side of it.

She didn't look as if she'd slept any better than Erin had. "Good morning. I don't suppose you've thought of anything."

"No. I'm sorry. What can I do to help now?"

"Well, stay off the subject with the other patients, for one thing. I'm sure they know something's up, but they don't quite know what it is. Dr. Brogan would prefer that the news isn't leaked out. Mr. Denton was a prominent man in this town, you know. His family is still prominent, and they won't want publicity any more than we do. Janet, you have patients to bathe, I think. Erin, come with me to Dr. Brogan's office, please."

There was nothing in Vonda's voice suggesting that Erin would be held accountable for anything, yet Erin's mouth was dry and she was aware of the increasing tempo of her pulse as she stepped into Dr. Brogan's office right behind the nursing supervisor.

Dr. Brogan looked as usual, sitting behind the massive desk with nothing on it but a slightly wilted carnation in its expensive vase. Every silvery wave was in place; he wore a blue suit with a pale blue shirt and a white brocade tie, and he looked up at them as he spoke into the telephone.

"Yes, of course, Mrs. Lundstrom. I understand perfectly how you feel. We here at Forest Hills feel the same way, I assure you. Yes, we'll do our best, and of course we'll be in touch as soon as there is any news."

He replaced the receiver and stared at the two women who had entered his office. "Upset, but not hysterical, thank God. Her husband had already gone to work, so I didn't have his reaction to contend with. I suspect he's going to be exasperated with the old man and furious with us for letting him escape."

Vonda sighed softly. "Well, I can't blame them. I take it the car didn't give anybody any hints of where it had been."

"Not unless you consider the fact that it apparently collided with one vehicle painted tan, another that was dark green, and a third that was yellow. There was a french fry on the front seat, indicating that he had something to eat, but that isn't much of a hint, either. Fast-food place, no doubt, but which one? Where?"

He pushed back his chair and stood up. "Erin, I'd like you to assemble the entire security force here in my office in an hour, including those who are off duty. *Especially* those who are off duty, the ones who were on when Mr. Denton walked away last night." For the first time there was a break in his composure; he actually ran a hand through the silver hair and left it standing in unruly peaks. "Damn it to hell, how could that decrepit old man get off these grounds without either of them being aware of it?"

"He's a sly old man," Vonda reminded him. "And he obviously plotted this out ahead of time. The notes about the movements of the staff members prove that. Apparently the security men follow a pattern, making certain rounds at specific times. Once he'd observed that, it wasn't too difficult to figure out the best time to walk out."

Matthew Brogan pinched the bridge of his nose as if to ease an ache there. "I wish someone had informed me sooner that food was missing from the kitchen."

"The cooks thought it was members of the staff," Vonda said, carefully neutral, "and no doubt hesitated to lodge a complaint that might have resulted in someone getting fired."

"I've never objected to the staff eating at night, or any other time," Brogan pointed out. He came around the desk, lifted the carnation out of the vase, and dropped it into his wastebasket. "The only way I'd fire anybody would be for stealing food to take home with them. Well, so far Mrs. Lundstrom agrees that we shouldn't call in the police. She doesn't want a story in the paper any more than we do. But if we don't find the old man, and quickly, that will change. Right now he hasn't been gone long enough to get her frightened. She's thinking about people discussing her senile old father, and embarrassed at what he might do to create a scene or a scandal. If he hasn't turned up by tomorrow, however, she'll begin to think something dreadful has happened to him, and insist on calling in the authorities. If she does, there isn't a hell of a lot I can do to stop her."

Erin didn't know where the impulse came from; certainly when she'd entered the office she'd intended no more than to speak when she was spoken to, and hope she'd be ignored altogether. And now, though the words came nervously, they were blurted out before she thought about them.

"Perhaps . . . I have a friend—an acquaintance—who used to be a police officer. He's a private detective, now, an investigator. Maybe someone like him would be able to help, without any of the publicity that could result from calling in the police. His name is Silas Copetti."

There was a small silence, broken when Vonda echoed the name. "Copetti? We had a patient by the name of Copetti."

Dr. Brogan was staring at her with no perceptible change of expression. "Yes, Isadore Copetti. He had cardiac problems. This fellow a relative?"

"Well, yes. A nephew." Too late Erin remembered Silas's warning: be careful about raising questions. It might be dangerous. Yet there was nothing here to suggest that bringing up Si's name could have any significance, and it did seem sensible to consider a private detective, under the circumstances.

Dr. Brogan rubbed thoughtfully at his chin. "Yes, well, we may come to that. You might get me this man's telephone number, just in case. In the meantime—"

A disembodied voice came over the public address system. "Dr. Brogan and Miss Busby, to room three-twelve, stat. Dr. Brogan and Miss Busby."

Erin jumped. Because it was a small hospital, and emergencies were few, the P.A. system was seldom used. Both Brogan and the R.N.s carried beepers while they were on duty, which drew far less unwanted attention.

Room three-twelve. "Mrs. Tosta," Erin and Vonda murmured simultaneously.

Erin was left standing there; the other two moved swiftly toward the elevator.

She went back to her own desk, her mind on whatever was happening up there in room 312. She placed the phone calls to the off-duty security officers and spoke to the ones on duty.

She couldn't help feeling uncomfortable about mentioning Silas after his warning about being careful what she said, but there was no way she could take the words back. She'd just have to tell him the next time she saw him.

If there was a next time.

The security men converged on Dr. Brogan's office as scheduled. They left the building twenty minutes later, not looking at Erin, their faces ranging from grim and white to red and angry. So Dr. Brogan was capable of harsh words and accusations. She wondered wryly if knowing that would make Silas feel better.

Just before lunchtime, Janet came by pushing Mrs. Hampton in a wheelchair. Erin looked up, trying to give the patient a bright smile. "Having an outing? It looks as if the sun might actually come out, doesn't it?"

"It's cold," Mrs. Hampton said sourly. "I hate fresh air when it's cold."

Behind the patient's back, Janet rolled her eyes, and mouthed the words, "Mrs. Tosta died."

Erin stared after them, distressed. Not unexpected, of course, but still. Mrs. Tosta had been a nice lady.

Another death. No doubt, Erin thought bitterly, Silas would make something of this one, too. Yet what could you expect?

She didn't know why she continued to feel so uneasy.

22.

In midafternoon the bingo game was in full progress. Erin could hear the laughter and the voices from the dining room down the hall, proving that not all the elderly patients were unhappy here, nor in distress.

She was scheduled to admit a new patient, and she had the papers all ready to be filled out and signed. She knew nothing about him other than his name: Richard Eldridge.

When the silver Rolls-Royce pulled up at the front door, and a uniformed chauffeur got out to open the car doors, Erin delayed making her next phone call to round up entertainment and waited for her patient to emerge.

There were two passengers: a beautifully dressed and coiffed woman in her late forties, and the most obese young man Erin had ever seen.

He didn't walk, he waddled. No expertise of an expensive tailor was enough to make him look well-dressed, though the gray pinstripe was of beautiful fabric. Erin hoped she was covering her reaction to so much fat on such a young man.

For he *was* young. He had a handsome face, but it was his eyes that would haunt her. He knew he was grotesque, and the knowledge was painful.

Ordinarily she would have offered a chair to the patient and any relative accompanying him while she did the paperwork. A glance at his bulk, and then at the chairs available, made it clear that this procedure would have to be varied today. No chair at hand could possibly hold his weight without splintering.

"Good afternoon," she said, keeping her voice pleasantly neutral. "Are you Mr. Eldridge?"

"That's right." Except for a slight panting from the exertion of walking to her desk from the car, his voice was almost seductively attractive. He had a wide, expressive mouth, a sensitive mouth. What must it be like, to be trapped in that mountain of fat?

"I'm Richie's mother," the woman said. "There won't be any publicity about this, will there?"

"Publicity?" Erin echoed. "No, of course not." She collected her wits. "Would you like to be seated, Mrs. Eldridge, while I get some answers to these questions? If you'd prefer, Mr. Eldridge, perhaps your mother could answer them, and I can get an aide to take you to your room."

"No, no," he said. "I can do it myself. I hope they're not going to put me to bed, anyway, are they? I'm not *sick*, you know. Just fat." He laughed, and it was one of the most melodious sounds she'd ever heard. It didn't go with the pain in the brown eyes.

He was only twenty-six years old, even younger than she'd thought. She hesitated over the statistics, then spoke in a normal tone. "Do you know your height and weight, sir?"

"Five-eleven, and four hundred and ten pounds. Give or take a few."

Erin swallowed and entered the information.

"What's all the laughter and shouting going on?" the young man wanted to know, waving one well-manicured hand toward the dining room.

"A bingo game. We usually have them once a week."

He nodded. "Sounds like they're having fun." He hesitated. "Am I the only . . . young one?"

"Most of our patients are elderly," Erin admitted.

His dark eyes were heavily fringed with black lashes. Beautiful eyes. "The treatment really works, does it?" he asked.

She didn't know what treatment he was referring to, and her uncertainty showed.

"The weight-loss program," he said. "That's why I'm here. We were told that this Dr. Brogan has some fantastic program for obesity, even for people who've tried everything else." He smiled; for a moment Erin thought she glimpsed the real man inside the unattractive hulk, and her heart went out to him. "I've tried everything else," he said simply.

He was, she learned, a disc jockey. Of course, with that voice, over the radio waves where he could only be heard and not seen— he'd be perfect.

"Naturally Richie doesn't have to work," Mrs. Eldridge informed her. "He didn't want to join his father and his brothers in the family business, Northwest Mining & Manufacturing, and so we didn't object when he wanted to occupy himself with this little radio job."

Why did she feel she had to belittle the radio job? Erin's gaze caught his, and she recognized the plea in his slight smile: *forgive this fatuous woman; she's my mother.*

"A lot of young people would give their eye teeth to be disc jockeys," she said. "If you'll sign here, Mr. Eldridge—"

He obliged, bending awkwardly to reach the papers on her desk. "Would it be too much to ask people to call me Richie? That's how I'm known on radio, Little Richie. I'm going to feel as if I have one foot in the grave if everybody addresses me as Mr. Eldridge."

It was the kind of statement people made all the time; why did Erin feel a shadow—no, a chill—pass over her?

"Of course, Richie. I'm Erin, Erin Randall. There now, here comes Janet. She'll show you to your room and get you squared away."

Mrs. Eldridge remained behind at Erin's desk. "They'll start treatment right away, won't they? How long do you think it will take, to get his weight down to what it ought to be?" She didn't wait for a reply, but added, "He weighed one hundred and eighty pounds when he was ten years old. We've taken him everywhere, and nobody's helped him. I do hope this Dr. Brogan is as good as they claim he is."

Erin didn't know what to say. For Richie's sake, she hoped so, too, but the young man presented a considerable challenge. "Let me call Dr. Brogan's office and see if he's free to talk to you now," she suggested, reaching for the phone.

She went back to work, looking up only when someone suddenly appeared beside her.

"Mrs. . . . Randall, is it?"

Erin lifted her head, taking in the white lab coat, the pale skin, the horn-rimmed glasses that were so thick they distorted his eyes.

"Oh, yes, Dr. Spaulding."

"I wonder if I could get you to do something for me. When you aren't tied up with your duties here, of course. I asked at the office, but they said it's the end of the month and they're billing and so on, that maybe you'd have more time."

"Yes, Doctor, what can I do for you?"

He put a folder on the corner of the desk, and she noticed his hands for the first time. Strong, well-shaped hands, with fine dark hair on the backs of them. Attractive, masculine hands, the only attractive thing about him.

"I need someone to pull the charts of all the patients listed here, and make copies of their statistic sheets. That's these things," he said, opening the folder. "There's one at the back of each chart. The nurses keep them up to date, so all that's necessary is to pull each one out, make a copy of it for me, and put the original back. Nothing difficult, only a little time-consuming."

"I'll be glad to do them for you. I'm just about finished here now. Shall I bring them over to the lab?"

"Yes, please. Thank you, Mrs. . . . Randall."

It was the first time she'd actually spoken to him. He seemed so vague, yet everyone said he was brilliant. Well, she thought, amused, there were more important things for him to store in his memory than the names of insignificant employees.

She took his folder to the office, where Evelyn McKay led her to the record room next door and explained how to find what she wanted. The Xerox machine was right there beside the door, and Evelyn made sure she knew how to operate it.

There were perhaps sixty-five or seventy names on the list, which was in alphabetical order. The charts were on shelves that ran along both sides of the small, narrow room, color coded to make them less likely to be misfiled.

The sheet she was to copy was easy to find. She glanced at the first one, noting that it seemed to be no more than a daily listing of T/P/R (temperature, pulse, respiration?), B/P (blood pressure) and weight, though that appeared to be checked twice a week rather than daily. Dull stuff for a brilliant doctor to work with, she thought.

She read the next name on the list and felt her breath catch in her throat. Isadore Felix Copetti, it said.

Silas's uncle. She hadn't wanted to think about Silas at all, and she had no intention of spying for him. She suddenly realized she didn't *want* to find anything suspicious. It was a good job, and she didn't want anything to spoil it.

She found Isadore Copetti's chart and removed the back sheet, putting it through the Xerox machine without looking at it. And in the few seconds that took, curiosity surfaced.

The sheet was so neatly laid out that it wasn't difficult to follow. When Uncle Isadore entered Forest Hills he had weighed 194 pounds. The last entry, written on the line above the single word *Expired* and the date, was 152 pounds.

A forty-two-pound weight loss, in a matter of less than four weeks?

Unconsciously, Erin frowned. *He* hadn't been admitted with a problem of obesity, had he? She turned back to the chart itself, to the form Sylvia had filled out when he entered the hospital. Isadore had stood five feet nine inches tall, so 194 pounds wasn't too far out of line.

Involuntarily, she scanned the rest of that admitting form. He'd arrived by ambulance from San Cristobal General, after a cholecystectomy—gallbladder, wasn't that what it meant? She flipped over into the nurse's progress notes. He'd come in with a temperature of 103.6; he'd had a fever because of a bladder infection, as far as she could figure out.

The memory was fresh. Dr. Brogan in his office this morning saying, "Isadore Copetti. He had cardiac problems."

Yet there was nothing in the initial notes indicating heart difficulties. The lines in her forehead deepening, Erin turned a page and read on.

Much of it was medical jargon, but she got the gist of it. He'd been weakened by surgery and infection, and had apparently been expected simply to convalesce at Forest Hills. After the first two days, his temperature had dropped into a normal range, and there were notations to the effect that he ate well. Fluid intake and output were recorded, seemingly adequate. Erin didn't know enough about what would be normal—especially measured in cc's —to be able to judge.

Nothing about cardiac problems. Nothing. She leafed through the pages more quickly. He hadn't even had much medication, as far as she could tell, and that was charted on a separate page, which made it easier to follow.

He'd had several injections of something designated as A.S. and on several occasions had had Demerol. The latter would have been for pain, no doubt. She couldn't find anything in the medical dictionary on the counter that seemed to correspond with A.S.

Maybe the mysterious A.S. was a heart stimulant, or regulator, or something. Only it seemed odd that there was no mention at all of any heart problem. She had no medical background, but even she knew that you monitored the heart with an electrocardiograph. If a man had heart trouble, wouldn't they monitor it in some way on a regular basis?

In spite of herself, Erin was troubled.

She turned back to the first chart she'd copied from, a Gladys Bornecker. Age 61, admitting weight 182, and at the end of the chart, weight 130. Beneath the final notation on weight, the word *Expired* and the date.

Since Mrs. Bornecker had been only five feet two, no doubt she had been too heavy. She might well have needed to lose fifty-two pounds. Still, it had been done rather rapidly. Erin had always understood that weight loss should be gradual, though perhaps when it was under a doctor's supervision, for a specific medical reason, that rule would not apply.

She glanced at her watch. She couldn't take the time to read all the charts, or she'd never be done before quitting time, and she'd had the impression that Dr. Spaulding wanted these as soon as possible.

On impulse, she ran the list of names through the Xerox, putting the duplicate list into the pocket of her jacket, feeling guilty as she did so. And then, still not fully understanding what she hoped to accomplish, nor why she did what she had sworn not to do, she copied the back sheet from Isadore Copetti's chart, and that from Gladys Bornecker's, and tried not to look at the figures on any of the others as she copied the rest.

23.

Aaron Spaulding stared at what he had scribbled in the hand that was nearly unreadable to anyone but himself.

Panic, horror, disbelief left him trembling in dismay.

He must have made a mistake somewhere, this couldn't be right. Somehow he'd miscalculated, he'd overlooked something.

He scrubbed his face with a crumpled handkerchief, gulped from the cup of lukewarm coffee that was always at his elbow, and gritted his teeth.

He'd go over the entire thing again.

An hour later, he slumped over the papers in despair.

The results were the same.

Matthew Brogan was in a foul humor. That damned old man had vanished into thin air, the Lundstroms were going to force him to call the police if they didn't find Denton in short order, and then the whole mess would be in the papers. While it was not all that unusual for a senile patient to wander away from a rest home, nobody had ever escaped from *this one* before, and it was hardly an advertisement for the place.

Denton hadn't gone home, so the other logical guesses would be that he'd found refuge with a friend (unlikely, since he didn't have many friends anymore; two were in rest homes, one had recently moved out-of-state to live with a daughter, and one was in San Cristobal General after fracturing a hip) or he'd holed up somewhere with strangers.

That meant hotels and motels. Brogan put Evelyn McKay to work calling those, concentrating on the ones within a two-mile radius of Forest Hills. Chances were the old man wouldn't have driven farther than that. Up to now Evelyn hadn't come up with anything.

He had a new patient that he hadn't yet had any time to evaluate, so the young man was simply sitting around waiting. Brogan had talked to the mother, putting her off by saying that he wanted Richie to have some tests before any treatment was started. Brogan had urged her to go home, promising to call her as soon as there was any information to relay, but she hadn't done it. She'd booked into the Seaside Hotel and would no doubt be bugging him until they started to get some results. Well, that, at least, was something Brogan could be reasonably sure of. The Eldridges were wealthy enough to pay for extended treatment, too.

The phone rang, and when he picked it up his ex-wife Karen was on the line. That was another thing he could always count on: if he was run ragged at the hospital, either Karen or Charlotte would bug him with complaints or demands.

"I'm up to my ears, Karen. Can you make it quick?"

Her voice was crisp. "Certainly. I'm busy, too. Meggie's gotten pregnant by that Nordland boy, the one with the pimples. Can you arrange for an abortion? Is that succinct enough for you?"

The news rocked him, literally, backward in his desk chair. "Are you sure?" He saw Meggie in his mind's eye, pretty, innocent, young. "My God, she's only fourteen!"

"Yes. Sarah has two friends who've had abortions at twelve. It's a difficult world, Matt. I don't want to keep you from your pressing business, but as long as I've managed to get through to you, I'd better unload it all. Sarah's been expelled from school, and the only place I've found that will take her is St. Gregory's. The tuition is sixteen hundred a month."

He made a strangled sound. "What happened?"

"Apparently she and another girl were caught with marijuana in their lockers. The police are not taking any action, beyond the dressing-down the judge gave both of them, but if it happens again it'll be a different story. St. Gregory's has very tight security."

He felt sick. What had happened to his little girls? His babies?

Karen was still talking. "I've already filled out the papers to get her in there. I assured them you'd take care of the bills. And speaking of bills, there's one more thing. When the workmen came to redo the floor in the downstairs powder room they discovered termites. They haven't spread extensively yet, but it'll probably cost about $6,500 to take care of it."

He watched his knuckles whiten on the arm of his chair. "For crissake, I hope that's the end of the good news."

"That's all for today. I'm sorry, Matt, I'm not enjoying this any more than you are."

"No," he said, with a frustration he could not conceal, "but at least you're not the one paying for it."

After he'd hung up he sat for a minute with his head in his hands. Damn it to hell, he was doing very well with the hospital and his practice, but there had to be an end to the drain on his funds.

There was a tap on his door, and Evelyn put her head around the edge of it. "I've found him, Doctor. Ernie Denton is registered at the Western Motel, on San Jacinto."

She handed him a slip of paper with the address of the motel written on it. "Do you want me to notify the Lundstroms, to go and get him?"

Brogan shoved back his chair. "No. I'll get him myself."

"And I didn't want to cut in on your phone call, but Dr. Spaulding wants to speak to you immediately. He said it's urgent. He asked that you go over to the laboratory."

Brogan was already moving past her. "He'll have to wait until I get back here with Mr. Denton."

"Do you want me to call Mr. Denton's family and tell them we know where he is?"

"No, I'll do that." He almost forgot, and had to turn back to say over his shoulder, "Thanks, Evelyn."

"Just give me the key, and I'll let myself in," Brogan said.

The motel manager hesitated. "You're not family, sir?"

"I've already told you," Brogan said, suppressing his irritation, "that I'm his doctor. He's old and sick, and he wandered away from my hospital. If you feel you must get authorization from his daughter, fine, but he's been without his medication long enough now that it is dangerous. I don't know Mrs. Lundstrom's number, but I suppose it's in the phone book. Or we can call my office for it. Only let's not delay any longer in getting Mr. Denton the medical attention he needs."

The manager sighed and reached behind him for the key. "Number fourteen," he said.

Brogan strode briskly along the narrow sidewalk and slid the key into the lock, easing the door open.

The sour odor in the room made him wince. Unconsciously, he held his breath as he approached the bed.

Ernie Denton sprawled on the shabby orange spread, asleep with his mouth open. He looked ghastly, with sagging skin and a poor color. Brogan checked his pulse and pushed back an eyelid. Ernie didn't rouse.

"Come on, Mr. Denton, wake up," Brogan said briskly, and slapped the old man lightly on the cheek. There was no response, and Brogan swore.

The wastebasket beside the bed overflowed with garbage and fast-food containers. An overturned milkshake and spread across the nightstand and dripped off onto the carpet, and the old man's shirt front was a mess of stains.

"Is . . . is he all right?"

Brogan spun to confront the manager, who stood in the doorway. No doubt he was concerned about a death in his ratty little establishment. Well, Brogan didn't want Ernie to die here, either. It would cause all kinds of complications.

"He's sick, and the quicker I get him back where he belongs, the better."

"You want me to call an ambulance?"

Brogan considered briefly. "No, it'll be quicker to take him myself, if we can get him into the car. I'll move it up here by the door, and perhaps you can help me get him on his feet."

Clearly the manager would rather have been left out of it—and who could blame him, considering what the old man smelled like, and weighed?—but he was anxious to be rid of this guest.

"Whatever you say," he agreed.

It took both of them, and by the time Ernie was in the back seat of the BMW, Brogan was sweating. He thanked the motel manager, slipped him a ten-dollar bill, and got away from the place with a decided feeling of relief.

"Clean him up before his daughter gets here," Brogan directed. "She's pretty agitated, especially after I told her he's semicomatose. I'm going home to shower and change; I'll be back to speak to Mrs. Lundstrom when she arrives."

At least if the old man died it would be here, not in a miserable motel room, he thought. This way he could sign the death certificate, and there wouldn't be anything messy about an autopsy, though he had no real reason to fear that a postmortem examination would reveal anything out of the ordinary.

He had just stepped out of the shower when he thought he heard the outside door open. He'd left it unlocked, he often did, since there was a security lock on the main door downstairs.

"Somebody there?" he called out, wrapping the towel around his hips.

"Matthew, I sent word I had to talk to you."

His brother-in-law appeared in the hallway, following him into the bedroom, where Brogan had laid out fresh clothes.

"Sorry, Aaron, I had a crisis. We found Ernie Denton in a seedy motel downtown, and I had to bring him back. What's up?"

"Matt, we're in terrible trouble."

For a few seconds the words didn't actually register. Brogan stepped into shorts and was holding a T-shirt when the sense of what Spaulding had said fully penetrated his consciousness.

"Trouble?" he echoed.

And then he looked at the other man and forgot about dressing.

"My God, what's the matter? You look awful! Are you sick?"

"Yes," Spaulding said. "I don't blame you, I should have used my own judgment. We should never have started the serum on human beings without further testing with the rats, and the rats didn't show . . ." He faltered, and Brogan, now completely alarmed, reached out to ease the other man into a chair.

"What? What's happened?"

Spaulding swallowed, and Brogan saw the tremor in his hands as they rested in his lap. "I've been over the data three times, and it still comes out the same." He gave a sort of choking sound. "To think I named it after Lisa, the Annalise Serum! My God, what an irony that is!"

Brogan restrained himself from shaking Aaron Spaulding's shoulder.

"Pull yourself together, man, it can't be that bad. What's it all about?"

Spaulding's eyes filled with tears. "It's not what we thought, at all, Matt. It . . . the effects of the serum are irreversible. It took so long to discover it because"—he choked again—"because it's a long-range thing, not a quick one, except for the initial effects. I've felt all along that what we were doing was wrong, that there was something I couldn't put my finger on, and at last I know what it is."

In a state of shock that now held him immobilized, Brogan stared at the other man and heard the words that made him feel as if the entire world were crumbling around him.

"The action of the serum doesn't stop, Matt," Spaulding said, and the tears spilled down his thin, pale cheeks. "Once the patient has had it, it keeps on working, even when we don't administer it anymore."

24.

"What are we going to do?" Spaulding demanded.

Brogan knotted his tie, glanced into the mirror while he ran a brush through his silvery waves, and turned to face his brother-in-law. "Well, not panicking would be a step in the right direction. Though that's a tall order, I'll admit. You're absolutely sure? There's no possibility of a mistake?"

"We made the mistake a long time ago. They're dying, Matt. All the people we gave it to, they're dying."

"Some of them would have died anyway," Brogan pointed out, wishing to Christ he could draw reassurance from his own words. Wishing he didn't feel sick and angry and afraid. He hadn't been this frightened since he was a kid, when he'd been cold and hungry and ill, while Lisa lay in a stupor with a raging fever and his mother hadn't come home for four days. He'd thought she was never going to come home again, and that his sister was going to die; at the age of nine he hadn't known what to do.

He didn't know now, either.

"We'll have to face the music," Spaulding said, his throat working. "Maybe someone else will be able to turn this thing around."

The inner fear and sickness and anger coalesced into a conviction. "No. We're not going to turn ourselves in and have the world blow up in our faces," Brogan said. "What the hell good would that do?" He shrugged into his jacket, and checked the mirror again. It was a link with sanity, keeping that outward appearance normal. It helped him believe that there was a way out of this mess.

Spaulding spread his pale hands in a helpless gesture. "What choice do we have? We can't keep on killing people!"

"Of course not. We'll stop the injections immediately."

He adjusted his cuff links and drew in a deep breath. "Come on, let's get out of the bedroom. We could both use a drink."

"How will a drink help?" Spaulding asked in despair. "It won't change anything."

"It'll calm us both down, and maybe we can plan. Nobody knows about this. It was an unfortunate mistake on our part, yes. But do you honestly think the world will be a better place if we both go to jail for manslaughter, or murder, or whatever they decide we're guilty of?" There was a savageness in his movements as he walked through to the kitchen and poured out stiff shots of Chivas Regal over ice, not bothering with water. He gulped his own and snorted impatiently when Spaulding left the other glass sitting on the table.

"We can't get away with it. Even if we stop now, we can't get away with it."

"How the hell do we know that at this stage of things?"

"Matt, be realistic. It'll be better all around if we admit what we've done and take the consequences—"

"Better for whom? Maybe it doesn't matter to you if you go to jail, lose your license, see the rest of your life go down the drain. I don't see it that way. I've got three kids, all of them needing a father, depending on my financial support—I've got the hospital, and I'm damned proud of it. What about all the people who are patients, and the staff here? What do you think it would do to all their lives? Where are the staff going to find new jobs? The R.N.s administered the serum, after the initial doses. Are they going to be dragged through court, too, to explain why they didn't know what it was, or what it did? What if some of them lose their licenses, too? There's not a damned thing we can do about the people who've died, but there's a reasonable chance we can salvage our own lives, and the lives of our staff."

"There are still the patients who've had the serum, who are continuing to lose weight." Spaulding sounded as if he were hollow.

"And every one of them is old, and has other problems that are going to kill them before long anyway."

"We don't know that. I mean, some of them might live years before they die—except for the serum. Don't we owe them something?"

A tiny rational part of Brogan's mind recognized that Spaulding's pessimism was justified. Yet he refused to buckle. Only a matter of hours ago, he'd had the world in his grasp. Oh, sure, there were problems, but if this damnable serum had turned out to be as fantastic as he'd thought, that alone would have made them both rich—and he'd have had everything else. Everything.

He'd be goddamned if he was going to let it go.

"We owe more to other people, including ourselves. Aaron, sit down. We need to talk."

Spaulding appeared not to have heard. "I'd rather have died than see anything like this happen. I wanted a memorial to Lisa, something to help other people like her—"

"Don't get maudlin on me. Lisa's gone, the others are gone, but we're still here. I feel bad about them, too, but there's nothing we can do to bring them back. We simply won't use the serum anymore, though I hope you'll continue the research—if it could speed up metabolism, there must be a way to make it cut back once it's achieved its objective in weight loss, and the potential will still be there—"

A shudder ran through Spaulding's gaunt frame. "I couldn't do anything more with it—"

"Not on humans, you damned fool, on your rats and rabbits!"

"I told you, it didn't work the same. The animals didn't die. Only the people died. Matthew, I can't live with this on my conscience. I'm going to call—"

He turned toward the wall phone over the counter, and Brogan moved with an alacrity he hadn't shown in years, adrenaline surging through him and bringing out sweat that left him instantly soaked.

"The hell you are! You're not calling anybody. For God's sake, sit down, and let's talk!"

"There's nothing to talk about. We've killed people, however inadvertently, and there are more in danger. Someone else might be able to help them—"

"If anybody else had anything like this ready to market, we'd have heard about it. We can't do any good by making this public, and we can do lots of harm. Aaron, damn it, I will not let you go off half-cocked and ruin us both!"

Under ordinary circumstances Spaulding would have been no match for Brogan. Yet there was a strength born of desperation in him now, as he lunged for the telephone.

Brogan grabbed him and then, when Spaulding continued to struggle, knocked him backward as hard as he could.

"Aaron, listen to me! A few minutes isn't going to make any difference, even a few hours—Aaron?"

His brother-in-law had slid down the wall and was sprawled, half-sitting, at the base of the cabinet beside the refrigerator. There was an expression of stunned surprise on the man's face—and something else that made Brogan catch his breath.

He'd seen death too many times not to recognize it.

"Oh, Christ! Aaron, what the hell—?"

Aaron was not going to reply. A hand that had only moments before been upheld to defend himself slid off his thigh onto the tiled floor.

Brogan reached for the limp wrist, searching for a pulse that was not there.

God Almighty, this couldn't be true. He'd been in the midst of a nightmare, and instead of going away, the nightmare was getting worse.

How could the man be dead? Brogan hadn't even struck him, he'd only shoved him—

Breathing heavily, he rose to his feet, and then he saw it. On the edge of the yellow Formica counter, a red stain.

He bent to turn Spaulding's head, far enough to see the wound nearly hidden in the lank hair. Though it didn't look like much, it had obviously been enough.

Brogan was still breathing noisily, but he was beginning to calm down. It was up to him, now, how he handled this mess. Only he and Aaron had known about the serum, and now there was only himself. Brogan began to pull himself together.

He stepped over Aaron's outstretched legs and reached for the phone.

While he waited for the aide car, Brogan stood for a moment staring at his reflection in the mirror, unconsciously straightening his tie. There was nothing to suggest there had been a struggle. Hell, maybe Aaron *had* died of a coronary.

He was aware of an inner tremor, but also of a sense of growing calm. He was used to emergencies, he'd learned years ago to think fast and act fast when he needed to, to save a life.

This time the life was his own, and he didn't intend to lose it.

25.

"You have to get the rest of them," Silas told her flatly.

Erin stared at him, torn between exasperation and a growing fear. "What're you talking about?"

He tapped the Xeroxed sheets with a forefinger. "You have two of them, two people who entered Forest Hills Hospital, lost a lot of weight, and died. We have to know if the same thing happened with the rest of the ones on that list."

"Why should you think that?" Erin asked, but her voice was not as forceful as it might have been.

His eyes were like pewter. "You had your own suspicions, or you wouldn't have copied these two. We need the rest of them, Erin."

"But there are sixty-eight names on the list! And I've finished the job they set for me to do. I have no reason to be in the records room at all, let alone long enough to copy a sheet out of each of sixty-six more charts!"

It was as if her words didn't register. "Two charts don't prove anything, except to add to my gut instinct that something is wrong in that place, but if the results are the same on the others—even you will have to admit that would be pretty damned strong evidence of something."

"There can't be anything wrong," Erin said in desperation. "They're caring, decent people. I know they are. They're concerned, and they're doing their best for their patients."

"Maybe. Maybe not. Erin, think about it. Think about what you can do to get those other charts. You're never going to be able to rest now, any more than I am, without knowing for sure."

It was true, yet she couldn't quite give in to it. What if there *was* something dreadful going on, something that would result in one of the people she worked with—or more than one—ending up in scandal and disgrace. Maybe further investigation would topple the entire institution, and her job with it.

Yet there was far more at stake than her job, crucial as that was from her own standpoint. Lives, possibly.

Her head ached. She had intended to wait until Silas contacted her, even wondering as she had whether he *would* call again.

Looking at him across her kitchen table, Erin knew that she was very strongly attracted to him. What she didn't know was how he really felt about her. All she could be certain of was that he'd known, before that lovely day in the park and the one on the beach, that she worked at Forest Hills, and that he'd approached her hoping to enlist her help in investigating the place.

He hadn't called, though he might have if she'd waited long enough. The trouble was, sitting at home looking over the papers she'd copied from hospital records, she'd been afraid.

Yes, afraid. And the fear had been building ever since she'd dialed his number and asked him to come over to see the records.

"You've done this job for Dr. Spaulding. Do another one," Silas said, not looking at her but at the papers before him.

"I can't," Erin said, but he hadn't stopped speaking and didn't seem to hear her.

"Tell the other women in the office that he's asked you to get some more pages copied. Why should they be alarmed by that? They'd probably rather have you do it than have any work added to what they're already doing."

"But Dr. Spaulding hasn't asked me to do anything else!"

"You think they'll be aware of that? You're the one who told them he'd asked you to do it this time. Why should they question it if you go back for more? The guy doesn't even talk to anybody, you said. He works out there in his laboratory and doesn't communicate with anybody else except, once in a while, with Dr. Brogan. I can't see where there's much risk in getting the rest of the charts; there's no reason to think anybody will compare notes and realize you're into the files without authorization."

"But what if they do?" There was a note of desperation in her words.

"And what if you don't do it?" Silas demanded. This time he stared directly into her face with an intensity that squelched, momentarily, what she'd been about to say. "If you're right, Erin, if nothing wrong is going on, what harm will you have done? But if somebody out there is killing people, and you *don't* do anything about it, are you going to be able to live with knowing you contributed to more deaths?"

"That's not fair," Erin protested, though the sinking feeling was enveloping her now.

He laughed, a sad, bitter sound. "You think life is fair, do you? At your age?" And then, becoming aware of how wretched she was, he relented a little and reached for her hands.

"Honey, I know you're not used to this kind of thing, and it's shaking you up. But you're the only one in a position to find out the truth. Think about it. It's not only that a number of people may have died because of something that shouldn't have killed them, but more may die if we don't interfere. Isn't that more important than any other consideration?"

He saw by her face that he'd touched a nerve, and tightened his grasp. "What is it? What did you remember?"

"Richie. Little Richie, he said they call him." She told him about the newest patient. "He's only twenty-six. And . . ." For a moment she couldn't say the words. "He came in to be treated for obesity."

"Obesity. Fat. Uncle Izzy lost forty-two pounds, about half of them he didn't need to lose. Mrs. Bornecker lost fifty-two pounds, which she maybe did need to lose. Mrs. Tosta was once heavy, had lost a lot so she looked good when she went home, and came back looking like a skeleton and died. When Sylvia went to work at Forest Hills, she was fat. She lost weight, and kept on losing, past the point where her boyfriend wanted her to stop dieting. Only she *wasn't* dieting. Did you find out if the former bookkeeper was once fat too?"

Erin shook her head. She felt numb. Was he right? It sounded convincing when he started summing things up, yet she knew the people at Forest Hills, she *liked* them. It was impossible that they were knowingly doing something to the patients that was causing their deaths.

"Is there any chance that Mrs. Masterson has a chart at the hospital? You said Dr. Brogan gave medical advice to his employees. He might have treated her. Look for her chart, too, with the rest of these, why don't you."

Erin swallowed. "It's already on the list. I didn't realize it until after I came home, so I didn't look at the chart."

Abruptly he released her hands and stood up. "Okay. Get the rest of these charts, first. Then we'll decide what to do. You want to make a bet that every one of them had a major weight loss while they were at Forest Hills?"

She rose, shaking her head. "No. But I don't understand it. Silas, I really don't see how I can go and copy all those pages. They're confidential and I have no right to them."

She knew he wouldn't accept that, and he didn't. It took him another ten minutes of persuasion to wear her down.

Perhaps it was true, that no one would question the matter if she said Dr. Spaulding has asked her to copy more charts. Yet the idea of doing it was terrifying.

"Just act as if you have a right to be in the records room," Silas advised, "and they'll never know the difference."

He grinned then and patted her shoulder. "Don't worry so much. Listen, I have to go. I'll call you tomorrow night. No, I'll just come over and see what you have. What do you say to another fast-food supper? I'll bring it along and we can go over the charts while we eat, so we won't waste any time."

"It sounds terribly romantic," Erin told him, trying for humor she didn't feel.

For a moment she thought he was going to reply to that in a serious vein, but the moment passed. "See you tomorrow," he said, and was gone.

As soon as he was out the door, the doubts swept over her again. And overlying the fear about the consequences of what was surely an illegal act was the uncertainty about Silas. He hadn't said anything more about marriage, and except for holding her hands across the table he'd made no gesture of affection.

Well, she thought defiantly, she'd decided she didn't want matters to get too heavy between them, hadn't she?

Unless, of course, he'd been serious. Did she care that much for him, enough to want to marry him?

She didn't know. Erin picked up their coffee cups and put them into the dishwasher. If he cared about her, would he ask her to jeopardize her job, to compromise her integrity, this way?

He'd warned her earlier that it might be dangerous to ask questions openly, yet now he wanted her to take overt action that surely was more dangerous still. He'd made no comment when she'd admitted that she'd offered his name as a private investigator to Dr. Brogan, only raising his eyebrows a trifle.

Suddenly, vividly, she remembered Richie Eldridge. His dark eyes, his words in that astonishing voice. "Am I the only . . . young one?" And "I've tried everything else."

What if Silas was right? What if something was happening at Forest Hills, something the staff might not even be aware of, that endangered Richie and the others?

She'd given way to Si's pressure because she was weaker-willed than he was, rather than from any conviction of her own that stealing records was a necessary and justifiable action. But as she moved about the kitchen, wiping up, setting the table for morning to allow an extra few minutes to sleep, Erin thought about Richie, and about Sylvia. Sylvia had been her friend, and Sylvia was dead.

She owed it to both of them to learn the truth. She knew that when she went to work the following day she'd be shaking in her boots, but she'd try to do what Silas had asked.

Erin was feeling mildly queasy when she left home the next morning, a sensation that increased as she approached the hospital. It would only get worse, she knew, until she'd accomplished the theft of the information on those sixty-six charts. Theft. It was not a word she'd ever thought of in connection with herself, and a scalding shame was added to the apprehension. Yet she tried to perform her duties as usual.

The moment she walked through the front door, she knew something important had happened. The patients seated around the lounge were talking in low voices, pausing when they saw her, then resuming the whispers.

Now what? Dry-mouthed, Erin spoke to one of the aides who was on her way off duty.

"Carol, has something happened?"

The girl paused, buttoning her coat. She, too, lowered her voice. "You haven't heard?"

"I just walked in. What is it?"

"Dr. Spaulding's dead. Heart attack, I guess, though they said he hit his head when he fell, so that may have been a contributing factor. Dr. Brogan's pretty shook up."

Consternation surged through her. How could she pretend to be doing work for Dr. Spaulding now?

"Oh, heavens. No wonder Doctor's upset. Dr. Spaulding didn't have anything directly to do with running the hospital though, did he?"

"No. But some of the patients are upset too. Not that they knew him all that well, some of them had never seen him at all. I suppose when you're old and thinking about the end of your own life, it's not very reassuring when someone younger than you are drops dead of a coronary. There's my ride, I'll see you tomorrow."

Erin stared after her, emotions churning. This definitely complicated things.

Two patients were being discharged that morning, and there was a flurry of activity. Janet, after taking Mrs. Camandona out to her son's car, paused at Erin's desk to talk. "Too bad about Dr. Spaulding, isn't it? He was only forty-eight."

"Yes. That's awfully young." Erin changed the subject. "I understand Richard Eldridge is going to be one of your patients."

"Yeah, now that Mrs. Camandona is gone. He seems real nice. It's a shame he's so heavy, isn't it?" Janet observed. "He'd be quite good-looking if it weren't for his weight. He has a very nice personality, and the most beautiful voice I ever heard."

"Yes," Erin agreed. "It is a shame. Maybe Dr. Brogan will be able to help him. He's helped so many people." Her heart suddenly hammering, she spoke in an offhand manner. "Sylvia, and Mrs. Masterson. How much weight were they able to lose?"

"Oh, I suppose Sylvia lost about forty pounds. I don't know about Mrs. Masterson, she never talked about her weight, but it was probably more than Sylvia lost. She looked great until she had that stroke."

So that part of Silas's guess was true: Mrs. Masterson was one of those who had gone from obese to slender too.

Janet looked around to make sure no one was listening, and lowered her voice to a confidential level. "Did you hear about Miss Busby's rampage this morning?"

"No. Now what?" For a moment Erin was afraid it might involve *her*, though there was no logical way that it could.

"God, is she mad! I don't blame her, really, but she was taking it out on the rest of us, and I don't think anybody on the staff stole her watch."

"Her watch? The one with the diamonds?"

"Yes. If it was me, I wouldn't dare wear one like that to work, knowing how valuable it is. She hadn't insured it yet."

"And it's missing?"

"She took it off and left it in the drawer at the nurses' station when she went to help Nell give Mr. Crowley a bath. The last time he knocked Nell down and nearly broke his own neck, falling in the shower. So Busby got that look she gets when she thinks you're whining about nothing—it's no cinch handling that old man, I'll tell you, I'm glad he's not *my* patient—and says, 'Do I have to show you how to handle him, Graves?' and Nell was scared enough of Mr. Crowley so she had guts enough to say, 'I'd sure appreciate it if you would.' So Busby whips off the watch and tucks it away, and they go bathe Mr. Crowley. Both of them got soaked. I guess the only one not under suspicion is Nell Graves, because she was right with Busby the whole time."

"Has anyone stolen anything around here before?" Erin asked. She was sorry about Vonda Busby's watch, but she was so nervous about the task that lay before her that she couldn't quite concentrate.

"Not really. Oh, some of the patients swipe things from each other once in a while, but we usually know who it is. Like, Mrs. Camandona, who just went home, she used to take Mrs. Ford's slippers. Swore they were hers, or that she'd just borrowed them, or something. They were big pink fuzzy ones, so it was easy to find them. Once they even got into a shoving match over it. But no, not real stealing."

What *she* would do would be real stealing. If she could figure out a way to do it.

26.

It was not, after all, so very difficult, except for the wear and tear on her nervous system.

The whole place was reacting to the death of Dr. Spaulding, even though no one had known him well. The fact of his dying, and in Dr. Brogan's apartment, had distressed their beloved physician; therefore, it distressed them.

If Erin simply walked into the records room and ran off the sheets she wanted, would anyone question her? Or would they just assume that she was getting the information for Dr. Brogan? And would they, subsequently, mention to Dr. Brogan that she'd done it?

Only the thought of Silas, waiting for her, and the responsibility she felt for Richie Eldridge and the other patients forced her on. Without that conviction that she'd be criminally negligent if she didn't follow through on this, she would never have managed to do it.

Evelyn and Lois looked up and smiled, not pausing in their work at the computer keyboards as Erin passed through the main office. She didn't know what her own smile looked like, though she couldn't imagine that it was convincing.

She had decided that unless someone specifically asked, she wouldn't offer an explanation of her presence in the records room. She was a bad liar. So if she simply walked in and started copying, there was a good chance (she hoped) that the other women would take it for granted that she was there on Dr. Brogan's business.

Her heart was thumping uncomfortably as she closed the door behind her and set swiftly to work. She deliberately didn't read any of the charts, trying to make her mind blank to the implications of what might be in them, and to the consequences if she were caught.

On impulse, she copied complete charts for Isadore Copetti and

Mrs. Masterson, with nurses' notes, Dr. Brogan's progress notes, and lab reports, for all that the latter were meaningless to her. They might be significant to someone else. And then, an afterthought, she looked for a chart on Sylvia and copied that too.

Erin put the copies into a manila file folder and turned off the light, emerging into the main office in the hope that both clerks would still be too busy to speak to her.

Lois, however, had just turned off her computer and stood up. "Lord, I'll be glad when this day is over," she said. "It's been rotten, starting off the way it did, hearing about Dr. Spaulding."

Erin held her breath, waiting for the question that didn't come.

Lois sipped from a can of diet soda. "Too bad we can't put everything on the computers, so there wouldn't be any copying to do, isn't it? If the nurses didn't have to fill in some forms by hand, everything could just be run off on the printer, but Dr. Brogan didn't think it was cost effective for us to transfer all that routine information to the computer. Thank heaven! Would you mind dropping this off at Doctor's office on your way past?"

She handed over a folder, and Erin took it and fled.

He wasn't in his office, so she was spared the discomfort of standing in front of him carrying her pilfered information. She had waited all day to get the records, partly because she didn't want to have the stuff lying around after it was copied, and partly because it had taken her that long to work up the nerve to do it.

She had brought a tote bag for the purpose of carrying away the sheets from the charts, but when she reached her desk Janet was there waiting to speak to her about books for two of the patients. Erin dared not put the papers down in front of her or into the tote bag, either. Instead, she stuck them hastily out of sight in a desk drawer and tried to concentrate on what Janet wanted.

The aide was inclined to linger, making idle conversation, and Erin wanted to scream at her "Go, go!" Yet she kept control over her voice and her face, until the time when Carol came along and said, "Mr. Eldridge is asking for you, Janet."

Erin sat the tote bag on her chair, opened the drawer, and scooped out the stack of papers. She put on her coat, gathered up bag and purse, and let herself out the front door. Across the parking lot, the security man lifted a hand in salute, and she waved back as she slid into the Camaro.

She was shaking, but she had the records Silas had asked for.

Silas took the news of Dr. Spaulding's death with a contemplative look. "I don't suppose he was taking his own serum, was he?"

Irritation touched her. "I wouldn't have any way of knowing that. From what everybody said it seems he had a heart attack and fell, striking his head on the corner of a counter. I never heard anything to suggest that he was ever fat."

"Well," Silas said, scowling and rubbing the back of his neck, "there are a couple of factors in common to all of the rest of them. The patients."

Erin nodded. "They were all overweight to begin with, and they each lost from forty to one hundred pounds over a relatively short period of time."

Silas stood up and refilled both their cups from the coffee pot plugged in on the counter. "And every one of them was given this mysterious A.S. Which we haven't found in any pharmaceutical listing." He poked at the *Physician's Desk Reference*, which he had borrowed from a pharmacist friend. "What the hell is it? It can't be coincidence, that they all had this stuff and they all had incredible weight losses. It's not that easy to lose weight, eating's like smoking, it's addictive. You can't just easily stop eating or smoking."

"There's something now to help you stop smoking," Erin said, welcoming even a momentary change of subject. "The security men were talking about it at lunch. It's a nicotine chewing gum that you have to get on prescription—Nicorette, I think it's called. Tom says it really works."

"No kidding?" Silas sipped at the coffee and regarded her thoughtfully. "I'll have to check with Doc Kimball and try some of it. Well, if they have a magic gum to kill the urge for nicotine, maybe Doctors Brogan and Spaulding developed a wondrous drug that will kill the appetite. Only that isn't what it does, is it? The patients eat well, but lose weight anyway. So how's it work? Speeds up the metabolism, maybe, so the calories are burned up faster than normal? Is that possible?"

"Dr. Spaulding was working on cancer research, they say," Erin offered, not knowing the answer. "Because his wife died of cancer."

Silas paced restlessly around the kitchen. "Very commendable. Completely understandable. He hadn't found the cancer cure yet, or we'd know about it. Nobody's going to sit on that kind of information, not once he's sure he's got it. It's going to make him famous, and probably rich, when he makes it available. But what if, in his research, he stumbles on something else that's valuable? What if he finds something that doesn't cure cancer, but speeds up the metabolism, enabling the patient to lose weight without dieting? Or something that coats the food so that it isn't digested and the calories go right on through?"

Erin wasn't sure how he was making these quantum leaps in reasoning, though what he said had a certain logic, she supposed. "But the same thing's true as of a cancer cure, isn't it? If they had something that worked so well, wouldn't it be worth nearly as much as a cancer cure? I mean, there are thousands of people dieting, struggling to lose weight. If there were some easy way to do it, it would be worth a fortune. Wouldn't it?"

"Yes, it would." He drained his cup and put it down. "When it was perfected and marketed, of course. That's not easy with a new drug, not if you go the approved route. Sometimes it takes years, which might make the discoverer take some shortcuts, I suppose. Like experimenting on human patients without their knowledge or consent. You said this Richie whatever-his-name-is came all the way from Idaho specifically for a weight-loss program? How did he hear about Dr. Brogan in that regard? His reputation here is just that he runs a rest home."

"Silas, we're doing a lot of guessing, and there's no way of knowing if any of it's true."

"Sure. I admit that. But you have to admit that it makes sense. You know, what might help more than anything else would be to get hold of some of that stuff—the A.S. mentioned in all these charts. If we could have it analyzed—"

Distress brought her out of her own chair, knocking it over with a sound that made her listen to see if it had disturbed Sammie, who was sleeping at the other end of the apartment. "Silas, don't ask me to do that. I couldn't, anyway. It's locked up with the other drugs, and I have no access to anything like that. Besides, it would be a felony, wouldn't it? I could go to jail for years for stealing drugs!"

"And Brogan could go to jail for years if I'm right," Silas said softly. "Say they stumbled on something that causes weight loss without starvation, and they decided to try it on the patients at their hospital. Illegally, it would have to be illegally—they'd never get authorization to experiment on patients until the stuff had pretty well checked out in laboratory tests on animals. Say they start this with genuine good intentions, believing they've got something incredibly valuable, and they want to benefit mankind. Fat causes hypertension, strokes, heart attacks, all kinds of things. So they think they're going to save the world and do untold good. Only it backfires. There's something wrong with this stuff that they don't discover until they've given it to a lot of people."

Erin held up her hands as if to fend off his extrapolations in a physical way. "You're jumping to conclusions all over the place!"

"Yes, I am. But it fits, doesn't it? Sylvia, according to that chart, was given this mysterious medication. She lost forty-one pounds. The last injection she got—it all seems to be by injection—was at least three months before she died. You said she wasn't dieting." He poked around among the sheets of paper until he found the ones pertaining to Sylvia and stabbed at the figures written there. "She weighed one hundred and thirty pounds the last time they weighed her, at the time she had the last shot. How much would you say she weighed when she killed herself?"

Erin felt as if the lump in her throat was becoming a permanent and painful part of her anatomy. "A hundred and five, maybe. At most a hundred and ten."

"Right. She was skin and bones. She had a fight with her boyfriend because he wanted her to stop losing weight—*only she couldn't stop.* So she killed herself. In the bathroom, maybe significantly. Do you suppose she stepped on the scales and found out she'd dropped another pound or two, and it scared or upset her so much she grabbed that belt and knotted it around her neck and stepped off the edge of the tub?"

"Don't. Please, don't."

"She was a nice girl. A girl who'd been fat for twenty-eight years, who started to lose weight and finally had her first boyfriend. She thought if she kept on losing weight she was going to lose Zack, too, and she couldn't bear it. Damm it, I may be guessing, but I'll bet I'm pretty close to the truth. You got any better ideas?"

Reluctantly, Erin shook her head. "No. But I can't believe Dr. Brogan or Dr. Spaulding would harm anyone."

"Still St. Dr. Brogan, huh? Well, he may be as altruistic as you think he is, but the results are the same. People are dying. Maybe the stuff puts too great a strain on their hearts or their livers or something. Hell, I'm no doctor, I don't know how it works. Maybe those doctors are so goddamned stupid they haven't realized yet that they're killing people. There's nothing in that chart to suggest that Sylvia came back and talked to Dr. Brogan about the fact that she kept on losing weight, though you'd have thought he'd have noticed that her clothes were falling off. I can understand that they might not have made the connection between their medication and the deaths when it was only old people. Old people die all the time. But what about the young ones? Sylvia, and even Mrs. Masterson, she wasn't old, and now this Richie? Do you know if they've started him on this A.S. yet?"

"No. I don't have anything to do with their charts. Those stay at the nurses' station as long as the patient remains in the hospital. They're put away in records only when the patient goes home—"

"Or dies," Silas finished for her. "Okay, what have we got? They have a drug that apparently works miracles with weight loss but it's deadly. Maybe they knew that, maybe they didn't. What if Spaulding took it himself, and that's what caused his heart attack? Anyway, that doesn't change the facts. As far as we know, we're the only ones who've tumbled to the fact that there's something wrong. And if we don't do something about it, we're going to be as guilty as Brogan when more people die."

She stared at him. "What are we going to do, then?"

"I'll be damned if I know," Silas said.

27.

Brogan remained cool and urbane under the questioning of Lieutenant Fogarty from the San Cristobal P.D.

"I knew you'd want to see the death certificate," Fogarty told him, sliding the document across Brogan's desk. The officer was a tall, thin man with a dark pencil-line mustache and fashionable brown-tinted glasses, not what Brogan would have expected in a policeman.

Brogan scanned the certificate. "No sign of coronary involvement. Death due to the head injury. God, how tragic! He was involved in some very significant research, and now I don't suppose anyone else could even pick up the threads and go on with it."

"Cancer research, was it?"

Brogan nodded. "Yes. My sister—his wife—died of cancer. It was an obsession with him, to find a cure, or better yet, something to prevent the disease."

Fogarty leaned back and crossed an ankle over the opposite knee. "I'd like to hear again just how it happened, Doctor. How he came to strike his head."

The tendril of fear that had formed in his gut when Erin ushered the lieutenant in writhed and expanded as Brogan leaned back in his own chair, feigning a casual air.

"I've told it several times, and I don't know that I can add to it. We were in my kitchen, discussing his research. He was disappointed that something hadn't panned out the way he'd hoped, and I encouraged him, as I've always done, to try again. That's what you do in research. Every time you reach a blind alley, you go back to the beginning and try a different route. I wasn't looking at him when it happened. I had my back to him because I was getting us each a cup of coffee, and I heard him fall. I assumed he'd had a seizure of some kind. He didn't have any cardiac problems that I knew of, but that's what I thought had happened, that he'd suffered a heart attack. He never took care of himself, didn't eat right or get enough sleep, and got no exercise whatever. I called immediately for an aide car, and did what I could for him, but by the time they got there, he was gone."

"You weren't at odds over his research? You didn't quarrel?"

"No, why should we have? I don't know a hell of a lot about the research end of things, to be blunt about it. I provide the laboratory and the money to keep him going; he does—did—all the work, which is out of my area of expertise. Even when he'd tell me what went wrong, I didn't really understand it, only that he was disappointed."

Fogarty rocked gently in his chair, lifting the front legs off the floor. Brogan fought the compulsion to ask him to stop it; it was an expensive chair, and he didn't want the legs broken on it.

"If it wasn't because of a seizure, I'm sure I don't know why he fell," Brogan said. "It was late in the day and there's a good chance he hadn't had anything but coffee all day. He couldn't be bothered to cook, so he ate his meals at the hospital. The cooks would probably know if he'd had anything since morning. He often got so absorbed in what he was doing that he forgot to eat." *Careful*, he cautioned himself, *don't overdo it*, but he couldn't help completing the thought. "It may simply have been because of vertigo—dizziness, you know, from lack of food."

Fogarty's tone was dry. "I know what vertigo means, Doctor. That's your only explanation, is it? He hadn't eaten so he got dizzy and fell, hard enough to crack his head and kill himself?"

Brogan brought himself forward to lean his forearms on the polished surface of the desk, allowing an expression of incredulity to form on his face. "My explanation? I've told you what occurred, Lieutenant. It isn't up to me to explain why Aaron died, is it? It just happened to be in my apartment, but whatever it was, it could have happened anywhere else. I hope you aren't suggesting that I am in any way to blame. I assure you that I'm not."

It was disconcerting that Fogarty only continued to rock, his gaze holding Brogan's. The doctor held back additional words that might have betrayed nervousness, waiting for the police officer to make the next move.

The words came too late to be totally reassuring. "Of course I'm not suggesting anything, Dr. Brogan. It's only that it would be helpful if we knew exactly why Dr. Spaulding fell. If you'd shoved him, for instance—"

Indignation and distress registered on Brogan's face. "That was not the case. You didn't find any bruises on him, nothing to suggest he'd suffered anything but a fall." He tapped the death certificate. "Surely the postmortem showed whether or not he'd eaten recently, and if he hadn't, severe dizziness could well have been the result. There is nothing to suggest it wasn't simply an accidental death."

"Nothing at all," Fogarty agreed, but there was something in the eyes behind the tinted glasses that sent a spasm through Brogan's already tight gut.

Brogan rose abruptly. "Well, if that's all for now, Lieutenant, I have patients to see."

Fogarty unfolded his long frame. "Yes. I appreciate the time you've given me." He took several steps toward the doorway, then paused. "No doubt we'll be meeting again, Doctor. Good-bye."

Brogan stared after him, willing his face to remain blank in case the son of a bitch turned back once more. Was that a threat? *We're not done with you yet, Brogan?*

Fogarty couldn't know anything. There was nothing to know. Aaron's death *had* been an accident. Yet the interlude with the police officer left him struggling to control any outward manifestation of his inward tension.

The phone rang and he picked it up. "Dr. Brogan here."

"Doctor," Vonda Busby said, "I think you'd better come. Mr. Denton's vital signs are deteriorating. His blood pressure is 70/52 and his—"

He cut through her words. "I'll be right there," he said, and hung up.

It wasn't because of the Annalise Serum, he told himself, moving along the carpeted corridor toward the elevator. Denton was an old man, whose obesity had put a terrible strain on his heart and lungs. No doubt he'd have died in any event, no matter what their treatment, or lack of it, had been.

He stood for a moment over the patient, then spoke to the nurse waiting beside him. "You'd better get his daughter on the phone.

I'll talk to her. I doubt that his family will want us to use heroic measures. After all, he's eighty-two."

"Yes, Doctor."

Vonda left the room, and Brogan swore silently. Damn Aaron, why couldn't the serum have been what they'd thought it was? It would have been the answer to all his dreams. Why, he'd believed in it enough so he'd have taken it himself, if he'd needed it.

Were the authorities suspicious of him? Seriously? But how could they be? He was a reputable physician, respected, with a spotless record. There was no motive for him to have harmed Aaron, wanted to get rid of him.

At least no motive *they* could know about.

He was safe, he told himself. All he had to do was keep still, hold to his story about Aaron's collapse. There wasn't a thing they could do to put any blame on *him*.

Ernie Denton expired at 9:07 A.M. By 9:10 there wasn't a soul in the hospital who didn't know about it.

The patients were not unduly disturbed by this death. The old man had deliberately alienated himself from the others; he had made no friends. There were no mourners beyond his daughter, Paula, who shook her head when asked if she wanted to view her father's body before it was taken to the mortuary.

"No. I think I'd rather"—here she choked and covered her mouth with a lace-edged handkerchief—"remember, *try* to remember him, the way he used to be. Before . . . all this."

Brogan nodded understandingly and patted her shoulder, turning her over to her husband, who had arrived moments after his wife. Above her head, Neal Lundstrom sent Brogan a silent message: *Good, it's finally over, and we're all better off.*

Erin watched them leave, then tried to bring her attention back to the matter of lining up activities for the following week. It was, however, difficult to concentrate.

Ernie Denton had been on the mysterious A.S. He'd been massively obese. He had, in fact, still been heavy when he was returned to Forest Hills after his wild escapade in the stolen car, though substantial weight loss was evident in the sagging skin and the ill fit of his garments.

He was eighty-two years old, she told herself; you can't be sure he died because they gave him that medication.

Yet she couldn't be sure that wasn't the cause of his death, either. He certainly hadn't seemed *sick* when he checked in.

"Good morning, Mrs. Randall. Erin. May I call you Erin?"

She looked up to see Richie Eldridge before her desk. "Oh, hello, Richie. Yes, of course. How are you feeling?"

The young man shrugged. "Well, no different from when I came in. Fat, you know. Just . . . fat. We're waiting on various lab results, and I'm scheduled for my complete examination this afternoon. Dr. Brogan apologized for taking so long to get around to it, but I know he's had a lot on his mind—his brother-in-law's death and everything—and after all, I don't expect to lose this flab overnight anyway."

He smiled at her, and Erin thought how right Janet was: he would be very attractive, if one only looked at his face, not his body. What would it be like to be encased in such a body, helpless to be rid of the fat that threatened both his life and the matter of living?

She smiled in return and wondered if it looked as false as it felt. "Is there something I can do for you, Richie?"

"Janet said there was a small library here somewhere. I didn't see it, but I thought you might point it out—"

"Oh yes, it's the second door on your left down the hallway. I can't testify to how good it is, but if there's anything specific you want, I can get it for you from the public library."

He thanked her and she forgot her appointment book as she followed his progress down the corridor.

He hadn't started on the special medication yet, but he might, by tomorrow. How dangerous was it, one dose? Would all be lost if he received even that first injection?

She actually opened her mouth to call after him, then brought her teeth together with an audible click. What could she say? Don't let him treat you? Go home, learn to live with being fat?

He'd come here in desperation, and she had nothing definite to offer him in the way of proof of the danger, only some stolen records that could send her to jail if Brogan found out she had them.

Erin swore and knocked over the coffee cup she'd forgotten was at her elbow, then swore again.

She didn't see how she could do anything to protect Richie or anyone else. Until, half an hour later when she entered Brogan's office with the list of the next week's activities for his approval, the doctor himself gave her what she—or Silas—wanted.

"Looks good. Thank you, Erin," he said, putting the list into a drawer after he'd glanced over it. "Oh, do you have a few minutes to spare?"

"Yes, of course," she said, somehow feeling guilty because he'd praised her for doing her job.

"Would you take this bottle of serum up to Miss Busby? Be sure to deliver it to her personally; it has to be locked up with the drugs, so I wouldn't want it sitting around where a patient might pick it up."

The phone rang and he answered it, forgetting Erin. She reached for the bottle he had indicated, on the corner of his desk, and stared at the label.

She was holding a container of the mysterious A.S.

28.

For a few moments her mind raced. Here it was, the substance Silas thought had killed his uncle and Sylvia and all the others. The one that might be used to cause Richie's death if the treatment was started tomorrow, as was apparently scheduled.

Erin walked out of Brogan's office, willing herself to think. She couldn't just appropriate the container and hand it over to Silas to have it analyzed. But could she take some out of the bottle? How? What would she put it in?

She entered the elevator and touched the button to activate it, not knowing what to do. The container was one of those with a top that could be penetrated by a hypodermic, allowing the fluid to be drawn into the needle without being exposed to possible contamination. She didn't see how to get the cap off without leaving some sign that it had been tampered with, and it didn't simply unscrew so she could pour some of the contents into another container.

The elevator stopped and Erin stepped off, feeling wildly that she *must* take advantage of this opportunity, yet unable to see how she could.

Vonda Busby was at the nurses' station, writing in a chart. She looked up when Erin, seeing no solution to the problem, paused before her.

"Yes, did you need something?"

"Dr. Brogan sent me up with this." Erin lifted the vial, feeling as guilty as if she'd already stolen it.

"Oh, yes. We're getting low."

She started to reach for it, then turned her head when one of the aides hurried along the hallway.

"Miss Busby, Mr. Nelson just fell in the bathroom. I need help."

Vonda rose at once, pulling a ring of keys from the pocket of her uniform. "Here, Erin, just put it on the top shelf in the medicine room. The key's marked. Is Mr. Nelson injured, do you think, Carol?"

They were gone, leaving Erin with a set of keys to the medication room, and holding the bottle of A.S.

There was no one around when she let herself into the cubicle, which held only a refrigerator and shelves with neatly labeled bottles of pills and various liquids. She felt as if she were a thief about to empty the bank vault.

There was a window in the door she closed behind her, one with wire inside the glass for additional security, and her actions would be visible to any viewer. But there was no one out there, and Vonda Busby would presumably be gone for a few minutes, until the fallen patient was gotten back into bed and they'd determined whether or not he was seriously injured. She should have time if she hurried.

Erin scanned the top shelf and found a bottle identical to the one in her hand, with a matching label. It held only a little of the fluid, and she stared at it. How much would Silas need in order to have it analyzed? Could she get away with removing a dose of it, or was it monitored, as she suspected, so closely that even a tiny bit would be missed?

And what could she put it in? She had no container of any kind, and there were no discarded ones in evidence.

Even as she was deciding that the entire thing was impossible, she saw the solution.

The disposable needles that were used for the injections were in a container right in front of her, individually wrapped. What more logical thing than to load one of the needles?

Erin picked up the nearly empty container, hesitated, then exchanged it for the full one. It would be less obvious that a few cc's were missing from the larger quantity.

She'd never filled a hypodermic before, and her fingers were shaking so that she was awkward. After a quick backward look to make sure she was still unobserved, Erin completed the action and slid the little plastic cap over the point of the needle. It seemed to her that the pocket of her jacket must surely reveal what she carried, but she'd done it.

She let herself out of the medication room and relocked the door. Vonda and Carol were still busy in Mr. Nelson's room, and she wasn't sure what to do with the keys. It wouldn't do to leave them lying on the desk.

Voices led her to the door of Richie Eldridge's room, where she found Janet deep in conversation with the patient. The aide turned swiftly when Erin spoke, her cheeks flaming.

"We were just talking," she said lamely.

Erin couldn't have cared less. "I have Miss Busby's keys, and she's busy with a patient who fell. Would you return them to her?"

"Sure," Janet agreed, accepting the ring. "Uh, I guess I'd better go, Richie."

Erin nearly ran to the elevator, feeling a little safer once she'd left the second floor. She was aware of Dr. Brogan in his office as she walked past his open doorway, not looking toward him.

No one was near her desk. Several of the patients were listening to music in the lounge, and two were playing cribbage. None of them paid any attention to her as she dialed Silas's home number.

There was no answer, so she looked up the number of the cab company. "Would you have him call this number as soon as possible?" she asked. "It's an emergency."

Now, she prayed, if only Si would call back when there was no one near the desk to overhear the conversation.

The quarter hour before he called was interminable. She saw Dr. Brogan emerge from his office, felt her abdominal muscles tighten, and then exhaled in relief when he turned in the opposite direction.

The phone rang. "Forest Hills," she answered it, and heard the familiar voice.

"Hi, what's up?"

"I have something for you," Erin said guardedly, though there was no reason to think anyone could hear her. "Can you come and get it? Right away?"

His hesitation was barely perceptible. "Sure. You're on lunch hour in twenty minutes or so, aren't you? Want to go out for something to eat?"

"No, I'd better not. I've never eaten off the premises at noon since I've been here, and I don't want anyone to wonder. I'll . . . I'll walk out front right at twelve, though, if you can get here that fast."

"See you then," Silas said, and hung up.

She watched the hands of her watch crawling slowly until it was time to meet him, feeling the pressure of the hypodermic needle against her thigh, wanting a drink of water to ease the dryness of her mouth but unwilling to leave her desk to get one.

"Great," Silas told her, slipping the needle into his own pocket. "I don't know how long it'll take to find out what this is, but I'll ask Harry to give it a high priority. Since we don't have a clue as to what we're looking for, it may take a while, though."

Now that she no longer carried the incriminating evidence, Erin felt a little better. Enough so to notice the difference in Silas.

"Has something—did you quit smoking?"

"I got the gum. Yeah, I smoked my last butt last night. So far the gum's working, but I haven't figured out what to do with my hands." He laughed a little, and Erin studied his face.

"It's more than that, isn't it? What's happened?"

"It hasn't actually happened, yet. But something might." He leaned against the battered bumper of the cab. "There's a headline in this morning's paper, about a guy by the name of Mitchum. He's the captain who left me holding the bag when they took his word against mine, and got me invited to resign from the force. I was lucky they didn't indict me, but this time he didn't have a patsy lined up. The grand jury indicted *him* yesterday."

She stared at him uncertainly. "Will that do anything to . . . clear you?"

"Well, officially, I don't need to be cleared, since I was never charged with anything. But it may mean a chance to get back on the department."

His casual tone didn't deceive her. This was important to him.

"Oh, Silas, I hope so."

"So do I. With a regular paycheck coming in again, maybe I could get out of that dump I'm living in. Buy another house. Think about living like a respectable citizen."

He didn't say anything about sharing the house, but Erin nodded, her own spirits rising. She turned to go. "I'd better join everybody else for lunch, or they'll be wondering. The staff usually eats at twelve-thirty."

She was halfway across the street when he called after her.

"Good job, Erin."

She waved back, smiling. The smile held until she reached the front entrance and met Dr. Brogan, who had just left the building. He stared after the taxi pulling out and making a U-turn in the street.

Did he realize who was driving the cab?

"Getting some fresh air?" he asked. There was nothing accusatory in his tone, nothing unusual in his countenance, yet Erin felt a surge of pure terror.

"Hello, Doctor." Her heart was thundering a warning, and she feared what her face might reveal. "Yes, it's a nice day, isn't it?"

Brogan nodded and lifted a hand in a farewell salute and headed toward his car, leaving Erin thinking she'd feel something like this if she'd just been struck by a truck.

No, she amended as she entered the front doors, she hadn't been struck. Yet.

The truck was bearing down on her at eighty miles an hour, and she didn't know if it had any brakes.

Joseph Stein pursed his lips as he looked at the watch and adjusted it in its deep-blue velvet case. He supposed it was a good thing he'd sold it himself, for had it been one of his salespeople there would have been a furor about the commission. He couldn't very well pay a commission on an item that had been returned for a full refund.

He was putting it back into the showcase when Mrs. Arbini came in, trailing her deceptively wimpy-looking husband. Deceptive, in spite of his small stature and bald head, because Mr. Arbini was a self-made millionaire. Millionaires didn't qualify as wimps in Joseph's book, no matter what they looked like. The Arbinis were among Stein & Stein's best customers.

Joseph smiled a greeting. "Good morning, Mrs. Arbini. Mr. Arbini."

The woman fingered the Alaskan coral necklace that showed at her throat where her mink coat was unfastened. "What was that you were just putting in that case, Mr. Stein? A watch?"

He drew it out again and extended it for her examination. "Yes. Exquisite, isn't it?"

Mrs. Arbini studied it at close range. "Very nice," she decided.

Joseph couldn't help himself. "Would you think it likely that a gentleman would return it because the lady to whom he'd given it didn't care for it?"

Mrs. Arbini's eyebrows rose. "Hardly!"

"Just so," agreed Joseph. Particularly since Dr. Brogan had not exchanged it for something else that might have been more to the lady's taste. Joseph preferred genuinely wealthy people who didn't have second thoughts over the price of things, to whom sales were more likely to be final. "What can I show you today?" he asked.

29.

Brogan was wearing his suede shoes again, so he followed the paved walk out to the laboratory instead of cutting across the lawn. He unlocked the door and stepped into the building, which was cold and smelled of death.

Christ, what was the matter with him? The lab was the same as it had always been. The fact that Spaulding was gone, was never coming back, didn't endow the place with a different atmosphere except in his own mind.

His own mind was churning as Brogan walked to the desk where Spaulding had done those final calculations, the ones that had catapulted them into disaster. Surprisingly, especially if the police had any suspicions about Aaron's death, no one had asked to see the lab or look through any of the materials here.

He hadn't even thought of it himself until that Lieutenant Fogarty had showed up. Had Spaulding left anything lying around that would be incriminating if the police got around to poking into it?

The desk looked as if Spaulding had risen from it moments before. A half cup of cold coffee sat just off center of stains it had left earlier on some of the papers scattered over the scarred surface. He'd leave that, Brogan decided. No sense in cleaning anything up, it could convey to an eventual investigator the impression that something might have been covered up, and he didn't want that.

He had come prepared with a pair of surgical gloves; if they ever dusted this place for fingerprints they wouldn't find any of Brogan's, except maybe on the knob that turned the radio off. He'd never understood how the man could concentrate with that Top Forty crap in the background. He smoothed the thin gloves over his fingers, and bent to examine the papers that cluttered every inch of the desktop.

A pencil, broken in half as if under stress, lay on a paper covered with meaningless figures. Brogan studied it and decided if he couldn't make anything of it, the chances were nobody else would. He'd leave everything that didn't increase the risk to himself.

A good many of the sheets of paper were familiar to him: the records kept in the back of each patient's chart. After a moment he realized they all bore notations about the weight loss and the administration of the Annalise Serum.

Brogan's hesitation was brief. Any professional who had a chance to look these over would question that medication. With such an ambiguous designation as A.S. he could probably think up some harmless thing it might represent—he'd better figure that one out before Fogarty came back, just in case—but why leave these records here to get anyone started looking in that direction? That notation, and the rather spectacular weight losses, would jump out at anyone who looked over all the records if they had any medical expertise at all.

Brogan began to gather them up and slide them into a dirty file folder he took out of the wastebasket. There was no reason why anyone should ever look at the charts themselves, no reason why anyone should be suspicious of any of the deaths of his patients even if they thought there was something fishy about Spaulding's death.

He didn't see anything else that might offer clues to an investigator. Brogan checked around the rest of the lab, making a mental note to arrange for the disposal of the animals still in the cages, and stripped off the gloves, putting them in his coat pocket. He considered taking the folder and the record sheets out to the incinerator behind the hospital, rejecting the idea almost as soon as it formed. No point in taking any additional risk. If anyone saw him they might question it later, since he'd never burned anything before.

He didn't really even want to be seen carrying the folder away from the lab, in case anyone remembered that if they were questioned later. At the last moment he concealed it inside his suit coat, holding it in place with his left arm while he relocked the door from the outside.

Mrs. Eldridge hailed him as he crossed the parking lot toward the front door. "Good morning, Doctor! How is my son today?"

He gave her his customary smile. "We're still in the evaluating stage, Mrs. Eldridge. Treatment hasn't actually begun. When it does, as a matter of fact, it would be better for him if you went home and left him alone for a few weeks, at least."

She bridled. "Why? What's going to happen that his mother can't know about?"

"Nothing that you can't know about, I assure you. In fact, I'll be happy to make weekly reports to you or your family physician. But having you here will put extra pressure on him, you know. Just the idea that he has to give you a progress report every time he sees you, perhaps when there's been no real progress, will be additionally stressful for him."

Her eyes narrowed. "There *will* be progress won't there? We came all this way because we'd been told you were so good at weight-loss problems, and Richard is so hopeful—"

He started to spread his hands in the universal gesture of *Who knows?*, remembering only just in time that he was holding the folder with his left elbow. "I'm a doctor, Mrs. Eldridge, not God. I will do what I can for your son. Here, let me hold the door for you."

He wanted to get away from the woman, and he was glad that she swept on past him and toward the elevator down the hall. What *was* he going to do about young Eldridge? He had no idea how to produce the serum, Spaulding had always done that, but there was enough of it on hand to give Eldridge what he wanted. If Aaron had been right, the man would go home and continue to lose weight, and eventually die from it—why the hell should he die? Why hadn't Spaulding been willing to keep working with it and find that out?—but there was no reason to think that anyone would trace his eventual death back to Brogan. He'd already taken care of the problem of stopping the medications for the other patients in a way that wouldn't make the staff suspicious—they thought the A.S. was a food supplement, and he couldn't simply discontinue it without someone wondering why. But he could keep a special bottle to use for Richard Eldridge.

Erin Randall was not at her desk when he reached it. She ran errands all over the hospital, so that wasn't unusual. When the phone rang, though, he hesitated.

It chimed persistently, and with a muffled grunt of exasperation —for he was a busy man and answering telephones was one of the things he paid other people to do—he picked it up.

"Good morning, Forest Hills," he said.

"Good morning," said a female voice. "This is Harold Eldridge's secretary in Boise. I'm trying to reach Mrs. Eldridge. Is she there?"

"She just went up to visit her son. If you'll hold—"

"Would you have her call me back at her convenience, instead? I'm not at the office, so will you take my number, please?"

"Certainly. Just a moment." Brogan moved around to the other side of the desk, reaching for a note pad, searching for a pencil, aware that the folder inside his jacket had shifted position. Damn it to hell, why wasn't there anything here to write with?

He never carried a pen; they tended to leak ink from time to time and ruined shirts and jackets. He depended on his staff to provide pens when they were necessary.

There was no writing implement on the desktop; no doubt Erin carried one with her. He jerked open the top drawer of the desk and fished out a pen, scribbling the number the secretary gave him.

He was about to return the pen to where he'd found it when he realized that something was caught at the back of the drawer; it made a rustling sound. He jerked the drawer all the way out and pulled the paper free.

Though it was crumpled and torn, he recognized it instantly.

For a matter of seconds, his breathing nearly stopped.

He wadded up the paper and carried it with him into his office, where he disposed of the file folder, the surgical gloves, and the record sheet he had found in Erin's desk, a sheet from the chart of a patient who had left the hospital months ago. A patient who had subsequently died.

The cleaning people would burn it all this afternoon, along with the rest of the trash.

He made his way along the corridor, pausing in the dining room for a cup of coffee, carrying it with him into the business office.

"Good morning, Doctor," Evelyn McKay said, and Lois Nelson echoed the greeting.

"Morning." Did he sound as strangled as he felt? No, they were both smiling, unconcerned. "I'd like duplicates of everything in Mrs. Camandona's chart. You're both busy, maybe Erin could do it. Does she know how to find the charts, use the duplicating machine?"

"Oh, yes," Lois assured him. "She ran off some stuff for Dr. Spaulding a couple of times."

He sipped at the coffee he didn't want, nearly scalding his mouth. "God, that's hot!" He hoped he'd covered any slip he might have made in facial expression. "All right. I'll tell her what I want."

As soon as he was out of the room, he got rid of the coffee. What had Aaron asked Erin Randall to copy? The record sheets he'd looked at and removed from Spaulding's desk? Had the damned woman read them and understood the significance of them?

Back in his office, he closed the door and retrieved the folder and the crumpled sheet from his wastebasket, smoothing out the latter to confirm the name of the patient. Then he went through the copies he'd taken from Spaulding's desk until he found the identical sheet there.

A sheen of perspiration appeared on his brow, and he wiped it carefully with a spotless handkerchief.

She had made copies for Spaulding, as requested. But those hadn't been the only copies she made. Had she duplicated them all, the whole list of patients who'd been on the Annalise Serum? Stuck them into the top drawer of her desk until she could get them out of the building?

If it hadn't been for this one copy that had stuck at the back of the drawer, if he hadn't answered that phone, he'd have been none the wiser about what could only be an abnormal interest in his charts. He had to assume she had the other charts, that the one he'd found had been left in the drawer by accident because it had caught there.

The decision was made without conscious reflection.

Erin Randall could not be allowed to threaten his future.

30.

Erin looked up in surprise as Bessie, a kitchen helper, put the mug of coffee down at her elbow.

"What's this? Curb service?" she asked, trying for a jocularity it was impossible to feel.

Bessie was a woman in her early forties, a divorcée working to support several kids. "Doctor's orders," she said cheerfully. "Things have been so difficult around here the past couple of days, we've been asked to give a little extra service so people don't run their legs off on errands like getting coffee. I got my cart here, with fresh cinnamon rolls, too."

"Oh. Well, thank you, Bessie. As long as nobody minds if we eat at our desks."

Actually, she'd have welcomed a chance to stand up and walk around; she was getting an ache in her neck and between her shoulder blades, as much from tension as from sitting there working over the upcoming schedule for the past hour. Yet in another way she was glad not to have to encounter anyone else in the dining room.

She couldn't sit and make casual conversation with anyone. Guilt and fear seesawed within her. Just about the time she'd justified to herself what she'd had to do, she'd slide off that pinnacle into further guilt, and the fear had tightened her stomach so that she felt half sick.

In fact, by the time she'd downed the coffee and pushed the unwanted roll aside, she was feeling bad enough so that she had to rest her head on the appointment book and the notes she'd been working with.

A sudden surge of vertigo left her weak and clammy. Lord, she really was letting this get to her. She wondered if she would make it through the remainder of the afternoon or if she'd better ask for the rest of the day off.

When she stood up her head spun so that she clutched for the edge of the desk to keep from falling.

Good grief, she actually *was* ill.

"Erin? You all right?"

There was a roaring in her ears, and when she tried to look at the speaker her vision was dimmed, blurred. "I . . . I think maybe I'd better go home," she said with an effort. "I seem to be . . . sick."

A firm masculine hand grasped her upper arm; the voice spoke crisply to someone else. "Bring a wheelchair before she falls. Hold on, we'll take care of you."

Alarm joined the vertigo, and she felt too terrible to resist. She was eased into the wheelchair, where she could easily have collapsed completely. What was wrong? This had to be more than just nerves—

For a matter of seconds her vision cleared and focused on the coffee cup on her desk. *The coffee! Oh, dear God, had there been something in the coffee?*

She forced her numbed tongue to speak. "I want to go home."

"You're in no shape to drive," Dr. Brogan said, sounding smooth and competent and solicitous, as he always did. "Why don't we just have you lie down for a bit, see if this goes away?"

"No," Erin protested. "Call—call me a cab to take me home."

It was as if she hadn't spoken. Brogan was giving orders to the aide. "Take her upstairs, tell Miss Busby to find her a room where she can rest for a bit. Just keep an eye on her. If there's any further trouble, call me."

Her feeble protests were useless. Erin wasn't even sure that anyone could hear them; she sounded like a mewling kitten. Tears slid down her cheeks, but that didn't stop her progress toward the elevator, briskly propelled by an aide used to obeying orders.

The vertigo was succeeded by nausea. Struggling to keep it under control made her break out in a cold sweat so that she was scarcely aware of the elevator doors closing and then, a minute or two later, reopening.

She heard their voices—Vonda Busby's and the aide's—and then someone thrust an emesis basin under her chin just in time. The episode left her icy cold and shaking and weak enough so that they had to help her out of the chair.

"I don't think you're supposed to put her to bed," someone said. "Just let her lie down for a while."

"Take off her shoes, and cover her with a blanket," Vonda said briskly. "Rinse out the basin, she may need it again. Erin, can you talk?"

Her teeth chattered. "Please—I want to go home."

"Well, better not until the worst of this has subsided. She may be getting the flu. Janet, you're the only one who's had contact with her. Maybe we'd better divide your patients between the other girls, and you stay away from them until we know what we're dealing with here. The last thing we need is a flu epidemic throughout the hospital."

It wasn't flu, Erin wanted to say, but she couldn't manage it. She needed the basin again.

"Can you give me any idea how long it'll take?" Silas asked, watching as the lab technician smelled the vial and examined the contents of it. "I know if it's something really exotic you can't just rattle it off, but—"

The technician shook his head. "Nothing exotic about this stuff."

"You mean you know what it is?"

"Looks like plain old Vitamin B-12 to me. Hang on a minute while I check it out to be sure, but I think that's what it is."

B-12? Silas paced restlessly while the man was gone. It didn't make sense that they'd have charted a simple vitamin product under a cryptic code name; nobody would see the charts except Brogan and his staff. And how the hell could Brogan kill anybody with B-12?

The results were definite a few minutes later. Silas stared at the technician, beginning to draw some conclusions.

"It can't be a vitamin. I mean, maybe this stuff is, but the *real* stuff can't be. Vitamin B-12 won't cause rapid weight loss, will it?"

The technician laughed and patted his own expanding middle. "Don't I wish! No way, Si." His eyes were bright with curiosity. "What's it all about?"

"I'll tell you when I find out," Silas said. "Thanks, Bob."

There was only one thing that made any sense, he decided in the elevator going down to the street level. The son of a bitch had switched serums.

His nerve ends were tingling in the way they did when he knew he was closing in on something important.

If Brogan had substituted something harmless for the serum that killed, it meant he *knew* that A.S. stuff was deadly.

And it might also mean that he'd deliberately given Erin a bottle of it to deliver because he was suspicious of her. Brogan could have set her up, and if he had, then she was in danger, right now. Because she was doing what Silas had asked her to do.

He drove over the speed limit, heading out toward Forest Hills, and then he came to a complete halt as the traffic ahead of him stopped moving. After a minute or two during which he drummed impatiently on the steering wheel and fished out another piece of the nicotine gum, he leaned out and yelled at the motorcycle cop coming from the opposite direction.

"What's going on?"

"Wreck," the cop replied. "Some junkie plowed through a bunch of kids crossing the street. It'll be a while before anybody gets through. We got four ambulances on the scene."

Silas swore and twisted to look back. He was pinned in, he couldn't move until the traffic did. He swore again and thought about Erin, hoping to God he was guessing wrong.

Brogan moved swiftly and efficiently, letting himself into Erin's apartment with her keys. He didn't even have to hunt very far for what he wanted. The records were there in a stack on her kitchen table. He gathered them up, made a cursory search for anything else that might be incriminating, and walked at a brisk pace back to his car, parked around the corner.

There was nothing to suggest that anyone but Erin Randall had seen the charts.

The vertigo and the nausea came and went in waves. Between the peaks, Erin tried to sit up, and was immediately assailed again so that she could only flop back on the pillow.

Emptying her stomach had perhaps helped a little, though. It seemed to her that the attacks were less violent.

She told herself to be still and try to think, to plan.

She had to get out of here. Every sense told her she was in danger. There had been something in the coffee, she was sure of it.

This reaction was much like she'd had in the past when she'd been given opiates or barbiturates. Her intolerance for those drugs had been established years ago; she'd learned not to allow anyone to prescribe them anymore.

She'd been nervous and tense, but she hadn't been sick until she'd drained the coffee cup. "Doctor's orders," Bessie had said, and the terrifying conviction grew within her. Bessie had spoken literally. Brogan had prepared a cup of coffee especially for her, and given it to Bessie to deliver. Chances were the kitchen worker had no idea it was any different from those she'd been told to take to other employees.

What had she done to give herself away? Had someone, after all, observed her activity in the medication room? But no one had moved in the corridor, she was certain of it.

Erin lay quietly, feeling a little better as long as she didn't move her head. She was under no illusions about being able to get up and walk out of here yet, but if she didn't . . .

Dear God, what did Brogan intend?

She didn't really have any illusions about that, either.

Si, she thought desperately. Si, find out what was in the needle. Find out, and come back. Don't wait for me to get home tonight, come back for me!

There was no reason to think he'd do anything of the sort. Erin blinked against the sting of tears.

"Maybe we'd better keep her under observation overnight, just to be sure," Brogan said. "I've asked Evelyn to make up a chart for her, to keep everything proper. It'll be up shortly. In the meantime, I'm going to give her an injection to settle her down."

He made it up himself. Vonda continued with her charting, turning when he came out of the medication room with the hypodermic in his hand, to say, "Mrs. Norman is complaining of chest pain. I've asked the girls to keep a close eye on her. Do you want to do another EKG?"

"Yes, why don't you do that? I'll go down and take a look at her, and you give this to Erin. I'll chart it when the folder comes up from the office. Then get the EKG on Mrs. Norman. Send it downstairs as soon as you have the reading."

He handed over the hypodermic and strode off down the corridor, and Vonda stood up. She glanced at her watch—her old one, the new, diamond-encrusted one had never showed up and she was certain one of the aides had taken it, damn them—and sighed. She'd be glad when her shift ended, and hoped it wouldn't be necessary to work overtime. She was tired.

Erin wished she had something to wash out her mouth. Janet hadn't brought the carafe of water that usually sat beside a patient's bed, and the bathroom was impossibly far away.

The slight sound brought her head around to the doorway, sending another flood of disagreeable sensation through her, but it wasn't as bad as it had been before. Maybe the vomiting was a blessing in disguise; she'd gotten rid of part of whatever had been in the coffee. She'd probably have been comatose by now if the stuff had all stayed in her system.

At least her head was clearing. Enough so that the sight of Vonda Busby, approaching the bed with a hypodermic in her hand, sent a new wave through her, this one of pure horror.

Vonda smiled. "Feeling a little better? Doctor ordered something that will help you over this; he wants to keep you under observation overnight, just to be on the safe side."

"No!" The word erupted out of her throat as if torn from her flesh. "No, I don't want to stay here, and I don't want any medication! I mean it, don't you touch me with that!"

Vonda registered astonishment. "What's wrong? This is just something to make you feel better. If you don't want to stay, I'll talk to Doctor about it. It's up to you, naturally. Yes, Carol, what is it?"

"It's Mrs. Norman," Carol said breathlessly. "Come quick!"

Vonda's hesitation was momentary. She had taken the plastic tip off the needle; now she replaced it and put the hypodermic down on the table that could be wheeled up over the foot of the bed if the patient needed to use it.

Then she turned and followed the aide at a trot.

Erin was bathed in icy perspiration. What was in the syringe? Was it the serum that had probably killed so many people already? Or was Brogan using something faster, more efficient, so that she'd never be able to tell anyone what she'd found?

It took a supreme effort. A life-or-death effort. Erin knew, as surely as she'd ever known anything, that if she allowed anyone to give her that injection, it would kill her. Somehow Dr. Brogan knew that she was gathering evidence against him, and he couldn't allow her to do that.

She dragged herself along the bed, nearly falling when she reached out for the table, causing the sickness to rise within her once more, but her fingers closed around the hypodermic.

She slid it under the blanket, knowing as she lay breathing heavily and willing the sickness to subside that she had only postponed the inevitable. More of whatever was in the syringe was still available in the medication room. They would prepare another injection when they learned this one had disappeared.

Yet it was the only hope she had.

She deliberately slowed her breathing, inhaling deeply, and tried to think.

For a few minutes, incredibly, she must have slept.

When Erin opened her eyes they were focusing fairly well and looked straight into the face of Matthew Brogan.

For the first time, his smile seemed false. "Well, how are you doing?"

She could not speak.

"Miss Busby give you the injection, did she? Making you feel better?"

Erin remained silent, but the roar of pulsing blood in her ears was loud, so loud.

In the distance she heard voices; she could not make out the words, but they sounded angry. Erin concentrated on the man before her, gaze shifting when he drew another hypodermic out of his jacket pocket.

"Just one more," he said genially, "and we'll have you all fixed up."

"No," Erin choked.

His face changed perceptibly. "Oh, yes, I think so," he said softly.

"It's illegal for you to treat a patient who doesn't want to be treated," Erin said foolishly. "I'm not senile like the others." The effort of speaking left her drenched once more in cold sweat.

His smile made her flesh crawl. "No, but you're nosy, Erin. You should have minded your own business. This won't hurt, I assure you. You'll simply go to sleep. I intended to do it the easy way, like the others, but you know too much, don't you? I can tell by your face. So it has to be fast. You're young for a heart attack, it would have been better if you'd had an accident. Unfortunately, there's no time for that."

He had taken the plastic cap off the tip of the syringe and he moved purposefully to the bed and reached for her arm with a firm, strong hand.

His hand was cold, his touch unbearable.

Erin tried to fling herself away from him; the movement sent the nausea and vertigo over her again. She was so weak! There was no way she could escape him, no way . . .

In the hallway the anger had escalated. She heard without understanding or caring when Vonda Busby cried, "Janet, call the security guards!"

"Call anybody you like, but I'm going to see Erin Randall," Silas said loudly. "Erin! Where are you?"

Silas! He was here, just down the corridor!

The knowledge lent her the additional strength she needed. Erin twisted, reaching under the blanket to withdraw the only weapon she had—the injection that had been intended for herself.

Brogan had straightened, half-turning toward the doorway, a scowl forming on his handsome face at the ruckus in the corridor. The few seconds delay gave her the only opportunity she was likely to get.

Erin jerked off the plastic cap and plunged the needle as deep and as hard as she could into the muscular arm exposed where his sleeve had ridden up, the arm that held her pinned to the bed.

Brogan yelped and stared down in disbelief at the needle still embedded in his wrist, involuntarily loosening his grip.

Erin screamed, "Silas!" and rolled over the opposite side of the bed. She fell hard and pain jolted through her, leaving her winded. A remote part of her mind told her to run, but the best she could do was to make it onto her hands and knees.

And then Silas was there, and Vonda Busby, and two aides; the room was full of people.

Silas shook off the hands that would have restrained him and knelt to help her up. When he realized he had to hold her because she couldn't stand, he locked an arm around her waist until he could ease her into the wheelchair that had been left in the room.

"I'm sorry, Doctor, he insisted on barging in here," Vonda said. "I've called for . . ."

Her words trailed off as she stared at the hypodermic buried in Brogan's wrist.

"Are you in on it, too?" Silas demanded of her. "Because if you're not, you'd better call the police."

Vonda's mouth worked soundlessly for a moment before she found her voice. "What . . . what's going on?"

Brogan jerked the needle out of his arm and faced his erstwhile victim. He sounded hoarse. "What was in it?" he demanded.

Erin swallowed hard. "Whatever you told Vonda to give me. She didn't inject it."

"I was called away," Vonda began, then stopped. "What's going on?" she asked again.

Brogan didn't reply. He stood there in visible shock, not even reacting to the two uniformed security guards who had appeared in the doorway.

Seeing that, Tom, the senior man, turned to Vonda Busby for instructions. "Janet said somebody busted in here." His eyes sought Silas, but his tone was tentative, because Silas didn't look like a man one would easily throw out. "You want us to get rid of him?" Silas was resting a hand on Erin's shoulder, a pressure and warmth that seemed to help her fight off the terrible weakness. He ignored the security people to ask, "Are you all right? What did he do to you?"

"It's wearing off, whatever he drugged me with, in the coffee," Erin managed. "He didn't get to give me the injection. He dropped the syringe on the floor; it rolled over there."

"Drugged?" Tom echoed, and his disbelief was written on every other countenance facing them, except for Brogan, who was holding his wrist as if it were broken. "Hey, what the hell's going on? Erin, did this guy assault you?"

"No, Silas probably saved my life by yelling my name," she said, reaching up to put her hand over the one on her shoulder. "It distracted Dr. Brogan enough so I could . . . give him the injection he'd intended for me."

"Sir?" Even in this confusion, Tom remembered who paid his

salary, though he had a gut-wrenching hunch that maybe that wouldn't continue to be the case. "Doctor?"

Silas let go of the chair. "You," he said, addressing Janet, "get me a big envelope. One big enough to hold that syringe. We're going to seal it up, and you're all going to sign that you saw it sealed. And then we'll find out what he intended to give Erin. My bet is, that alone will convict him of attempted murder."

No one moved, except Janet. Shock waves ran around the room. Wordless, they watched as Silas retrieved the dropped syringe and sealed it in the envelope Janet brought. Each of them obediently signed their names across the envelope after Silas had sealed it and handed it over to Tom.

"I'm going to get Erin to a real doctor and make sure she's all right. It ought to be possible to find out what the hell Brogan gave her. I'd suggest that you call the police—ask for Lieutenant Fogarty, of Homicide."

Tom licked his lips. "I think maybe I better know a little more than I know so far, before I do that." His gaze flicked at Brogan. Unaware, the doctor was watching Erin, his shoulders sagging, his face suddenly gaunt. Tom saw no help there. "What am I supposed to say to the cops?"

"For openers, you can say he tried to kill Erin," Silas told him grimly. "And once we're sure she's going to be okay, we'll get to them with the rest of the story. About how Brogan and Dr. Spaulding gave a lot of their patients some mysterious serum they developed that caused a lot of them to die."

Vonda Busby exhaled the breath she'd been holding. "Oh, my God," she whispered. "The son of a bitch, whatever it was, he had *me* giving the injections."

"You mean it's true?" Tom asked uncertainly. "He—" The thought was so monstrous he couldn't put it into words.

"I don't know," Vonda said, "but you'd better call the police, the way the man says, and let them find out."

Silas grasped the handles of the wheelchair and headed for the door. Everybody melted away from him; no one tried to stop them.

"You got a regular doctor?" Silas asked as the door closed and the elevator started downward.

"I'll be all right. I'm feeling much better already, really I am. Most drugs make me throw up, and I didn't retain all of it—"

"I want you to have a blood test and a urinalysis before the rest of it's out of your system," he said, sounding grim. "I want to be able to prove in court what the bastard gave you."

"Oh." She hadn't thought of that. "Well, I guess that's reasonable. Oh, God, Si, I thought he was going to kill me! You can't imagine how I felt when I heard your voice!"

"I thought he was going to kill you, too. The 'serum' you swiped was nothing but vitamin B-12. Harmless. So I knew he'd switched it on you. How'd he get onto you?"

"I don't know. He *knew*, though. He told me—" She choked, repeating what Brogan had said about how she had to die quickly.

The elevator door slid open, revealing the ground-floor corridor, but Silas didn't step out.

"I got caught in a traffic jam, I was afraid I'd get here too late," he said.

She twisted her head to look up at him, ignoring the giddiness the motion caused. "I had no reason to think you'd rescue me. I just prayed. If you hadn't yelled my name, so he—he was distracted for a minute—"

"I realized something," Silas told her softly, "while I was stuck in that damned traffic. That it would be my fault if anything happened to you in this place. And that I wasn't kidding about moving from friends to engaged, and on beyond that as soon as possible. I don't know yet whether I'm going to be a cop again or not, or have a regular paycheck. And my guess is that you're among the unemployed. But I know a judge who'd waive the waiting period for a marriage license."

He'd moved around so she didn't have to strain to look into his face. "God knows what our financial prospects are. Maybe pretty good, maybe not. But I know what the *emotional* prospects are. And I hope you need me as much as I need you."

Tears formed in Erin's eyes. She clutched at the hands he offered, squeezing hard.

"Hey! You people getting off, or going up, or what?"

Silas swiveled to look into the wrinkled old face of Mr. Campton, the patient from room 280.

"We're getting off," Silas told him, and then, glancing at Erin for confirmation, "and going to see a doctor, and then a judge. The judge can even marry us, if you like."

He waited, watching her face, then wiped gently at the tears that spilled over. "Today?" he asked. "So neither of us has to go home alone tonight?"

Erin nodded, unable to speak, knowing it wasn't necessary.

Mr. Campton's face split in a wide grin. "Well, congratulations!" he said.

Brogan hadn't noticed the others leave. He stood alone in the room where only the rumpled bed gave any hint of the drama that had just been played out here.

No one had spoken to him. Not even Vonda Busby, though the look she'd cast in his direction had been eloquent.

It was over. There was nothing else he could think of to do, not with all the evidence they would have against him.

Bitterness was a scalding wave. He'd been so close to getting away with it, to covering his tracks and going on without Spaulding or the Annalise Serum he'd had such high hopes for. Nobody would believe that he hadn't intended harm to anyone, not the patients, not to Spaulding, not to anyone. Well, maybe to that interfering Randall bitch.

Did the stuff work, was it irreversible, right from the first dose? Brogan wondered dully. It seemed to him that he could already feel it, speeding up his metabolism, racing him toward the finish line.

ABOUT THE AUTHOR

WILLO DAVIS ROBERTS has written over seventy novels, including THE SNIPER, ACT OF FEAR, and THE JAUBERT RING. She lives in Granite Falls, Washington, with her husband, David, who is also a writer/photographer.